"When Love Calls"

by

L. A. Smith

Other titles by L.A. Smith

"Love 'n My Time"

"Making Love Last"

"Tattered Obsessions"

"When Love Calls"

Anthologies

"Rendezvous: Guiltless Pleasures"

"Two Timers"

e-books short stories

"Pearl Necklace"

"Eat'n Ain't Cheat'n"

Library of Congress Control Number: 2011960107

ISBN: 978-0-9776377-6-8
Printed in the United States of America
First Printing

Cover design by CoverMe Designs

For more information or to order additional
books, please contact:
Black Angle Publishers
Bowie, Maryland 20716
www.blkangle.com
www.authorlasmith.com

Prologue

Who would have imagined such a young, beautiful person with a bright future would be so emotional and tragically end her life, while at the same time causing so much pain for so many others?

KC was treated and released from Doctor's Hospital the night of the accident. DaRon had to stay overnight because of head injuries. With that large bump on his forehead, the doctors feared he could have sustained a concussion.

A single mother and her five-year-old daughter were admitted with multiple injuries. Someone's husband and father driving his daily route suffered fractured ribs, and one of the two sisters on the way home from a day at the mall had to be medevaced to the emergency room.

Chance and KC were in the waiting room with MacKenzie, DaRon's parents, and Mrs. Carter, KC's mother. As soon as they were allowed visitation,

MacKenzie was the first to go to her husband's room. DaRon's parents soon followed her. Chance and KC stayed in the waiting room consoling Joelle, who was an emotional wreck. The detective investigating the accident wanted to speak with KC alone, but he let the detective know that Chance was his business partner and a good friend. Neva Majuave was pronounced dead at the scene. When her parents rushed through the doors, a nurse immediately took them to a private room away from everyone to deliver the bad news. Everyone's heart went out to her parents as they all watched her father hold onto his sobbing wife while the two of them followed the nurse.

"Let's go in to see him," Chance said to them once the Mitchells returned to the waiting room.

"He's still sleeping. I believe MacKenzie's intending to stay through the night. Don't let her. We're heading home now," Mr. Mitchell said before shaking hands with KC and then Chance.

When the three of them walked inside his room, MacKenzie was seated in the chair next to his bed with her head resting on DaRon's hand. His eyes were closed and a bandage covered one side of his head. KC stood motionless by the door as Chance walked over to MacKenzie, lifting her from the chair. She sobbed uncontrollably in his arms. KC looked at Joelee and saw tears gathered in her eyes after seeing MacKenzie's distraught state.

"Buttercup…Buttercup! Sweetheart, listen to me." Chance held her cheeks with both hands. "He's going to be okay. It may be as simple as a mild concussion. He's going to be alright."

"Look at him. He's so helpless," she said between sniffles.

"He's sedated. We'll stay here with you until he wakes up, okay?"

She shook her head.

"Joelee," MacKenzie called to her before extending an arm. The two embraced, and then Joelee wiped her tears away.

"Stop it, girl." Joelee chuckled slightly. "You're making me cry. Come, let's sit." MacKenzie sat on the edge of the bed, and Joelee sat in the chair holding DaRon's hand. Chance and KC stood by the door.

"Do you know what happened?" MacKenzie asked without taking her eyes off of DaRon.

"It was a multi-vehicle accident. I'm not sure of all the details," KC answered, as he glanced down the hallway, expecting to see Neva's parents walk out any moment.

MacKenzie looked at Chance and asked, "Why was KC driving your car?"

"It's a company-owned vehicle," Chance answered without looking at her.

"That you park in your garage and drive every day! That's your car, Chance."

Although the vehicle was registered to Keon-Chance Technologies, Chance drove the vehicle as his own as KC drove his as his own. "KC needed to run an errand, and because I had his car blocked in, I tossed him my keys. For convenience, we park in the alley between the two buildings. It's no big deal Mac. It happens all the time."

"Run an errand? Run an errand, Chance? Is that the best you can do?" MacKenzie was sceptical. She didn't believe his answer.

"Don't do this Mac, okay?" Joelee said, attempting to prevent an argument, but mostly in her husband's defense.

"Look, Buttercup, I know you're upset," Chance said to her, "but this isn't the time to question his intent. Nor is it the time to drill me on something I know very little about."

"I'm sorry, Chance." She paused before saying, "Is everyone okay? The other drivers I mean?"

"I don't know that." Chance's response was short. He then looked at KC, knowing it wasn't the right time to tell MacKenzie that the vehicle he was driving slammed into Neva as she stood outside of it, killing her instantly. What she didn't need to hear was what her husband was doing with his former lover, the same lover who had shouted obscenities during the start of their wedding. However, the truth about the accident would soon come out, and as always, KC knew Chance would be there to mend any wounded hearts.

KC motioned for Chance to join him outside of the room without further conversation.

9

"What's going on, KC?" MacKenzie's question went unanswered as the two friends walked out of the room. She looked at Joelee as if she had all the answers, but in actuality, Chance had only told his wife the surface of DaRon and KC's involvement with Neva.

This was Chance's opportunity to hear the entire story of how Neva intentionally caused the mishap that resulted in the injury of four other drivers and ultimately her death. His persona changed drastically, and it showed on his face. Outside of the brotherhood, no one may ever know what happened between the three of them that caused that "company-owned vehicle" to be involved in the five-car pileup, resulting in the death of a mutual friend.

When the two walked back in the room, Chance had a sour look. Both Joelee and MacKenzie watched the two of them as they stood in the corner of the room in complete silence. Soon, DaRon stirred and slowly opened his eyes.

"Hi," MacKenzie beamed as she whispered.

"Hey you," he said back to her and then turned to Joelee. "Jo? What's with all the sad faces?" He lifted

10

his hand that she had been holding onto and kissed her fingers. "Give me some sugar," he told MacKenzie.

"We were so worried about you," she said after kissing his lips.

"How're you feeling dude?" Chance asked him as they both walked closer to the bed.

"I'm good." He reached for his head. "Ouch! I think."

The attending physician entered the room carrying a clipboard and began asking him a series of questions. Joelee stood between her husband and KC once they returned to the back of the room out of the way of the medical staff. After taking his temperature and giving MacKenzie his final diagnosis, the physician left the room. They all were relieved to hear that DaRon suffered no internal injuries and would be released in the morning.

When they returned to his bedside, KC reached out for a handshake and then leaned into DaRon, simulating a shoulder tap.

"It's all good, potna," DaRon said.

11

"Baby, do you remember what happened?" MacKenzie asked him.

"Naw, but I know this fool can't drive," he replied, referring to KCs driving skills.

The comment caused him to chuckle at his friend's comment. "We got lucky, didn't we?"

"I'll say. Yeah, real lucky. Was anybody else lucky besides us? Did anybody get hurt? I mean besides me, who else got hurt?"

"You don't remember?" KC asked.

"Man, I ain't seen nothing. All I know is we were having coffee..." He looked at Chance and then at MacKenzie. "Hey, babe, let me talk to these two for a minute."

"No. No, DaRon. Whatever anybody have to say, they can say it now."

Chance looked at Joelee and said, "Momma C is in the waiting room. Why don't you and Mac let her know that DaRon's okay and that we're talking," Chance said.

"Mac, let's give the guys some time to talk, okay? It's only fair with all that's happened."

"No, I think it's only fair—"

"And my momma thinks it's only fair—"

"Stop!" Chance was irritated and held his hand towards KC. "Joelee, take Mac to the waiting room and wait there with Momma C. Let her know that KC will be staying with her for a few days."

"Man, how you gonna..." KC smacked his lips before turning away. MacKenzie finally agreed and left the room. "...tell me where I'm staying."

Then he saw Neva's parents walk past the room. Her father had gathered his composure, but her mother was still distraught. KC peeped through the door in time to see the couple walk past the waiting room and through the retracting doors. Both MacKenzie and Joelee looked up to see what had caught his attention.

"KC!" Chance called out to him, breaking his focus. "You want to do this?"

After clearing his throat, KC asked DaRon, "What about this whole thing do you remember?"

"We were at JP's waiting on Neva. Man, she was crying and all. When we left the lot and got on the freeway, she was there. I remember she was standing there, like halfway in the HOV lane. When Mario

13

Andretti here…," he pointed at KC and then paused. "Where is she?"

KC shoved both hands inside his pant pockets and stood at the side of the bed next to Chance before explaining the fate of his former lover, their mutual friend. DaRon stared up at the ceiling with tears in his eyes, and when Joelee and MacKenzie returned, they noticed the moods had changed drastically. MacKenzie immediately went to her husband's bedside and sat.

"Baby, what's the matter?"

He didn't answer. Instead, he turned his head in the opposite direction to where Chance and KC stood with folded arms. Simultaneously, they both looked at him.

This time, it was MacKenzie and Joelee who wanted answers as to why DaRon's mood went from jovial to gloomy. However, in reality, neither one of them would tell Joelee nor MacKenzie about Neva being killed in the accident.

Joelee looked at KC as if she knew one of them had told DaRon that four other people were badly injured. Yet, DaRon's mood had changed because the

14

woman he once loved committed suicide by causing that four-car pileup when she stood in front of that company-owned vehicle that KC was driving. DaRon would never admit his strong feelings for Neva, but they all knew how he felt about her in college and probably days before his wedding.

MacKenzie stood and walked towards the door, then stopped. When she turned around, she had a perplexed look as she pointed in the direction of the retracting doors—the same doors that the distraught couple who KC had been watching walked through.

"That was... Was that couple that left..." She wasn't making a lot of sense as she tried to put all the pieces together. "Was that Neva's parents that left through the doors, crying?" she aimed her question at KC, but before he could answer, Chance stepped forward.

"Mac, please calm down."

"I will not calm down until someone tell me what the hell is going on. Were that couple Neva's parents? That couple that you were staring at, KC?" No one said anything. "Answer me!" she yelled.

Almost in a whisper, Chance instructed, "Have a seat."

Since she ignored his request, Chance pulled the chair away from the bed, slid it across the floor, and forced her to sit. He squatted to make eye contact.

"Before the accident, there was a misunderstanding. Because of it, I wanted DaRon and KC to meet with Neva to apologize for mistreating her."

"Mistreating her?"

"Yes. Before the wedding, they did some things to her, and when I found out, I wanted them to apologize, thinking it would end the phone calls and stalking."

"She's been calling—"

"Not him, but my wife and me. I spoke with her. Today's meeting didn't go like we thought it would. Apparently, Neva thought she could beg, cry, and plead her way back into his life." Chance paused before saying, "KC was able to stop the car in time, but the cars travelling behind him couldn't. She intentionally took her life by standing in the middle of oncoming vehicles on the freeway."

16

"DaRon?" Her voice was almost inaudible. "Why couldn't you tell me about this? About whatever was going on with you and Neva? We said we'd be open with each other." Then MacKenzie turned her attention to Joelee.

"Jo, she was your girl, your matron of honor. What's going on?"

MacKenzie looked to Joelee as if she knew of some involvement between her husband and Neva. Slowly, Joelee mouthed two words: *I'm sorry*.

MacKenzie then turned back to DaRon and said, "You betrayed me, DaRon. You all did." Then she slumped in the chair as they all watched the tears roll down her cheeks.

DaRon never looked her way until she spoke, and once he did, tears began to fill his eyes, as well. Chance stood over MacKenzie, staring down at her and rubbing her shoulders. KC stared at the floor, wishing this would all somehow go away.

Then KC reached for Joelee's hand without once looking her way. She, too, couldn't control her tears, and in that moment, no one spoke a word or moved a

17

muscle. The room had an eerie silence, and it was as if the entire hospital staff was giving them a moment of silence so they could weep in their own way for whatever the reason. And they all did.

Chapter 1

After pressing the ignore button, sending her husband's phone calls directly to voice for the third time today, Joelee looked at MacKenzie who had a grip on her own cell phone and was staring into space. She had made Joelee promise to not tell Chance, her husband or anyone else where they were staying. Joelee knew that MacKenzie had every right to storm out of her house in anger after the incident at the hospital. Understandably, MacKenzie felt betrayed by DaRon because he had not been completely honest with her during their short marriage. And that was the one thing MacKenzie ever asked from her husband. Even when they were students at the University, the one thing she asked for was honesty, and now she was doubting that DaRon had ever been honest in their entire relationship. Not only was she furious with him but she was furious with KC for being an accomplice to her husband's tryst with his ex-girlfriend Neva Maujava. The ex that followed and confronted them at the bridal shop; the ex that hurled obscenities at him during their wedding. As Joelee contemplated the events, she wouldn't blame her in the least because KC hasn't gotten over being the biggest player and womanizer she had ever seen. In actuality, it didn't happen the way MacKenzie assumed but Joelee knew she was too stubborn to listen to reason. MacKenzie didn't even listen to Chance when he tried to explain what happened that day Neva committed suicide. She surely didn't listen to KC when he made an attempt to explain the events because before he could even get one word out, MacKenzie slapped him across his face so hard the sound startled Joelee as the force of it caused KC to stumble backwards. Yeah, MacKenzie was indeed a scorned woman.

Unlike the previous night when she was too furious to talk and certainly too upset to sleep, MacKenzie needed to get off her chest what had been holding her down for hours.

"I'm so stupid. How could I be so stupid?"

"You're not stupid. You're in love and your husband loves you back."

MacKenzie hesitated and then added, "Ya know he introduced me to her." Joelee appeared shocked. "Yeah." MacKenzie let out a sarcastic chuckle and then continued, "My first year at the university, but after that day, I never saw her. I never saw them together."

"That's because they weren't. Maybe before the two of you got together. DaRon loves you. He would never hurt you Mac."

"How can you say that? Honestly? I'm not so sure anymore. After this, I'm not even sure my marriage is salvageable."

"It is. You guys need to dig down deep and make this work."

MacKenzie turned away signalling the end of the conversation and the two women once again sat inside the hotel room in complete silence for another hour before Joelee spoke.

"I'm going to call him back," Joelee said to MacKenzie as she sat on the bed now staring at her phone. She'd turned it off during the drive to the

Doubletree. Instead of driving to BWI as MacKenzie originally planned, Joelee convinced her to take some time to think about the situation and to stay at the hotel. After much relenting, MacKenzie finally gave in. She looked at Joelee and without saying a word her eyes told Joelee to keep their whereabouts a secret. Joelee said, "It's been three days, and I miss him, Mac."

But what surprised Joelee is when MacKenzie responded, "Me too, Joelee." Chance had always treated MacKenzie as if she were his little sister and as MacKenzie grew older, they became good friends. Joelee knew the words that came out of her mouth towards him three nights ago were only said in anger.

"Hey, babe." His voice was a concerned whisper when Chance answered the phone.

"I wanna let you know that we're okay. Mac is going to need some time. You know..."

"I know that, babe. Her and DaRon have to work on their marriage. But listen, I don't want what's happened to them to affect us. That has nothing to do with you and me." He paused and Joelee heard him responding to a voice that sounded like it was DaRon.

She had no words for her husband, but then he said, "I miss you."

"I know Chance, and I miss you too." Joelee looked at Mac to see her mouthing the words *tell him I missed him too*. And she did.

"Hey, babe, let me talk to her." Joelee handed her the phone, but she waved it away.

"That's not a good idea right now," Joelee said to Chance.

"You know I've been worried about you two. We all have been concerned. Where are you?" he asked, but it hurt her thinking that she couldn't say because of her promise to Mackenzie. And as if reading her thoughts, he said, "You may have made a promise to her but I'm your husband and we promised a lifetime of honesty, faithfulness and trust."

"I know," Joelee whispered. "But don't do this right now, alright? I'll talk to her again and call you back."

"Hey babe, I want you to understand something. I want you home because as my wife that's where you belong. And not somewhere holed up with-with. Look babe, DaRon's been trying to call MacKenzie and I know she has her phone. She needs to turn it on or come home and deal with her situation like an adult. He did nothing wrong. And I know for a fact that he did not betray her, nor did he step outside the boundaries of their marriage. Talk to her babe. Three days is enough punishment for everybody. Come home."

"I love you so much," Joelee said to her husband before ending the call. Then she turned to MacKenzie and said, "Let's go home."

Chapter 2

When KC pulled his vehicle into the parking lot of his complex, Parker was standing at the security door. He had just gotten his head handed to him by Chance, his friend and business partner, and had earlier been slapped by the wife of his other friend for arranging a rendezvous between her husband and his former lover. Now to see Parker, a former lover, standing at the entrance did very little to uplift his already diminishing attitude.

He was not in the mood for another confrontation with her. The last time he tossed her out of his apartment because she snooped around in his things while he was in the shower. He didn't care that she found the receipt for the ring he purchased, what he cared about was her invading his privacy. She had the nerve to yell at him because of it. Parker was only one of the many females he was seeing. There was nothing serious with her or any other woman.

KC asked, "Why are you camped out at my door?" He was about to walk away but chose to stay. What he didn't need was for her to cause a scene for the nosey neighbors to witness.

"You won't talk to me." And then Parker whined. "Why haven't you returned my calls?"

Irritated he responded, "You left ten voice mail messages on my cell phone. That shit is uncalled for, don't you think?"

"And!" she yelled.

"What are you, psycho? One message is enough, don't you think Parker? Who does some crazy shit like that? And what's with the constant text messages, huh? Damn!"

"What am I supposed to do when you ignore me? Huh KC? Huh? What do you want me to do?"

"Go home and wait until I feel like putting up with your bullshit ass attitude. But right now is not a good time for this crap from you."

"Where do you think you get the audacity talking to me any kind of way you see fit? I've been honest with you from the very beginning of our relationship and this is the thanks I get. And now you go behind my back and buy a ring for some chick."

While KC was in the shower, Parker took the opportunity to nosey around his bedroom. Inside one of his pockets, she found a receipt for an expensive ring. KC had purchased it after a meeting he and Chance had in the Tyson's area. In addition to cufflinks for himself, he'd purchased the ring for Shaeterra as a makeup gift. It was pricey, but worth every dime.

"Some chick...You don't have a clue what you're talking about."

"What I know is, I'm not the one with the ring."

"Parker, it's none of your business what I do, where I go, and how I spend my money."

"What KC? Did you think we were going to keep going back and forth in this relationship without having a commitment? Is that the way you envisioned us?"

"Yes." He was growing tired of the conversation and was hoping it would end with his short response.

"What am I, a dry-run to you?"

"Call it for what it is, because I'm not ready for a commitment."

"When will you be ready?"

"The question isn't when will I be ready, it's who will I be ready to commit to."

"I'm not good enough?"

"You're confrontational, vindictive, jealous of my friends, and I'm not going to deal with your mood swings."

"That's it, I'm through with you. You don't deserve to have me KC, and I was too blinded by your charm to see the truth. If you don't respect me for the person I am and can not give me the love I'm giving you, that's too bad for you. Fuck it! And fuck you for wasting my time. I deserve better from the man I'm in love with than what you're giving me."

Parker raised her hand as if she was about to land an opened palm across his face, but for KC, one smack a week was more than enough. He reached for it and held her tightly by her wrist.

"Trust me Parker, you do not want to put your hands on me cause as much of a gentleman I am, I'd still beat the living shit outta you if you did. I'm not in the mood for this bullshit."

She snatched her hand away from his grasp and turned and walked away. KC punched in the code to open the security door to his condo.

Chapter 3

Taleed was driving on 97N when his cell phone vibrated. He looked down at the display, to see that it was Candice calling. He answered, "Yo, whassup?"

"I'm going to a movie and having dinner with a friend of mine and was wondering if you could keep little Taleed for a few hours." He was shocked to hear Candice mention going out with a friend. She'd never mentioned having any friends in the DMV to hang out with.

"Damn Candice, you couldn't give me heads up like when I was there three days ago? Right now, I'm a good forty five--maybe an hour away from you."

"I'll wait for you, and besides it was a last minute thing."

After loudly breathing a sigh of frustration, he said, "I'm on my way." Then he took the next exit to get on to the secondary road heading towards her home.

Oh hell the fuck no. It seems like every time I turn around some muthafucka try to test my patience. Taleed thought. When he walked inside Candice's apartment to retrieve their son, he saw his worst nightmare. There he was, sitting on the couch flipping through the channels of the flat screen that Taleed had purchased three months ago, looking as if he owned the place.

"Ah, hell no! Hell muthafucking no!" Taleed said with extra bass to his voice. Nicolas looked away from the TV. "What the hell is his ass doing here?" Taleed asked Candice not once taking his eyes off of Nicolas. The last time they saw each other was a few months back in North Carolina when Taleed was stomping his size fifteen Timberlands in Nicolas' ribcage. It was an ass whooping well deserved since Nicolas had the nerve to snatch the phone from Candice when Taleed was trying to talk to her. Then Taleed later discovered Nicolas put his hands on her. He did not like hearing that at all because the next time, it could just as well be his son getting hit.

"Nicolas came up for a visit last night. We're going out," Candice said as if she was oblivious to the hate Taleed had for Nicolas.

"Last night? What do you mean last night? You telling me his ass stayed here last night?" Nicolas was quiet because he didn't want the confrontation with Taleed.

"Yeah. He *is* my friend, Taleed."

"Well for all I care, your *friend* can stay at the Quality Inn down the street. You think I pay the bills up in this joint for this mutherfucker to be lying up in here, flipping channels?"

Finally, Nicolas spoke up and said, "Candice, can we—"

"Shut the fuck up!" Taleed spat and then leaped towards him. Candice stood in front of Taleed and with both hands pressed on his chest trying to prevent him from bashing in Nicolas' face. If Taleed really wanted to swing on Nicolas, he could have easily tossed Candice's small frame to the side.

"Taleed, Taleed," she repeated his name.

"One more word and I'm about five seconds away from kicking your scrawny ass, muthafucka!"

Then Taleed pointed his middle finger at Nicolas and said, "That's that ass whooping you gon get for putting your hands on her. Bet!" Nicolas cowarded down. Taleed pushed Candice out of his way and stomped towards his son's room.

The younger Taleed was sucking on his two fingers while peacefully sleeping. Taleed pulled his hand away from his son's mouth, shook him and said, "Hey, boy. Wake up." When young Taleed sat up rubbing his eyes, Taleed reached for his over night bag and tossed a few items inside, then he scooped up his son from the bed and walked back in the living room.

Without stopping or looking at anyone in particular he said, "Your ass better be gone when I come back." In actuality, Taleed had no intentions of coming back to this part of town, at least not this night.

There were two things wrong with Nicolas being there. One is Taleed didn't like him, nor did he like the idea of paying the bills at the apartment and having another man reap the benefits. Another reason is Taleed felt that Candice deserved better.

After securing his son inside his car seat, Taleed sat behind the wheel and retrieved his cell phone.

"Yo man, I need a solid," he said after hearing his greeting. "I got a job to do, and I need to drop off my son." He started the car and drove the ten mile stretch to DaRon's home. Then he got a text from Candice that said:

`thx for ruining my date. Nic left`

A wicked smile spread across his face as he snickered feeling somewhat relieved to spoil the date she'd planned with her boyfriend. Taleed didn't like him and wanted him out of the picture. He texted her back:

`u can do better.`

Chapter 4

There aren't many women KC had a genuine interest in, but there was something different about Shaeterra Rice. Things didn't end well the last time they spoke, and KC wanted to make peace with her. It was important that he made peace with her. Not only was DaRon riding him about it, MacKenzie gave him an ear full because she felt he had mistreated her friend. After leaving two messages on her cell phone, Shaeterra finally returned his call and agreed to meet him at the apartment that she shared with two of her friends.

When KC steered his vehicle into the apartment complex, Shaeterra was about to get inside her car. He rolled down the passenger window.

"Hey! Where you going?"

She held up her gym bag and said, "It's time to do laundry."

"Take a ride with me."

"Where?"

"Get in Shae," he said before placing the car in park. KC exited the vehicle and opened the passenger's door. She stared at him. "Sit. I have to get back to the office in an hour."

KC drove in silence to the neighborhood park that was only five minutes from her apartment. He parked the car in the first available spot.

"You're really sweet Shae, and I like you. I value your friendship," KC said after helping her exit the vehicle. They walked down the foot trail and stood facing the man-made pond.

"You could have fooled me KC. For some odd reason, I opened up to you because I felt like I could trust you. I even shared something very personal with you. I don't know why but you turned this into a player's game and abused my friendship."

"No I didn't." KC had a sheepish look. Then he said, "It was a simple misunderstanding. I mean, I ain't never met anyone like you. I mean a woman like you." KC stuffed both hands in his pant pockets. He didn't know how to put the words nicely so MacKenzie helped him.

"You mean a virgin?"

"Yes!"

KC was used to having his way with women and thought that she would be no different. He'd never dated a virgin before and hoped not to ever have to encounter one. He should have known but it surprised him when one evening in his condo, she dismissed his advances.

"I'm not like the women you hang out with, and besides, I'm a little younger."

"That's what I didn't take into consideration. Your age."

"It doesn't matter."

"It does to me Shae."

"No, not really." She folded her arms across her chest. "I've forgotten about it already."

"Stop that. Listen to me please. I let you wear my pinky ring because you were looking at it and I thought you were going to jack me for it." She smiled at his humor.

"But for real, how was I supposed to know that you'd take it as a prelude to marriage?"

"Because I told you I wanted to be married and, and not in a meaningless relationship. There's a difference, KC."

"I know Shae, but last month when you gave it back, I wanted to tell you why I asked for it back and you were so pissed you wouldn't even listen."

Sounding defeated she said, "You took her to see your mother."

"No sweetheart, I did not. I was having dinner with my parents and Mom's would've been asking where the ring was. I haven't taken it off since she gave it to me."

"Oh." She unfolded her arms from her chest. "I didn't know."

"See, Shae, you didn't give me a chance to exchange my ring for this one." KC reached inside the front pocket for the Paloma's Tenderness ring he purchased almost six weeks prior. She stared at it before gently taking it from the palm of his hand. "I do value your friendship, Shae. This is a show of my appreciation of your friendship. I may not be ready for marriage but I want you as my friend from this day on."

40

"Ahh, KC—"

"What? You need help putting it on? I know it fits." KC took the ring from her and reached for her left hand. "It would make me happy if you accept this ring as a symbolism of our friendship." He slipped the ring on her finger and pulled her body into his.

"It's beautiful, KC." Then he wrapped his arms around her in an embrace.

"Just like the woman I'm holding. You're very beautiful, Shae." Then slowly KC inhaled her scent. He liked her warmth. KC closed his eyes and could feel his own body temperature raise a notch. She felt good in his embrace. *Man what I would give for–*

Shaeterra broke into his lustful thoughts, "Does your girlfriend know about you giving me this ring?"

"Um," slowly opening his eyes, KC pushed away and said, "Shae, I don't have a girlfriend." He turned her body away from his and began retracing their steps back towards his vehicle. "Right now, it's just you and me, baby." The two walked arm-in-arm, retracing their steps back to his vehicle.

During the drive back to her apartment complex, Shaeterra tightly held his hand in her lap. She was constantly admiring her newly acquired jewelry. When KC walked her inside the apartment he leaned in for a kiss. Shaeterra didn't object. Her lips were soft and warm. Sweet gardenia fused the air. KC once again inhaled her fragrance before playfully pecking at her lips. It was a turn on and he desperately wanted to be inside the warmth of her softness. Since that wasn't happening he pulled himself away, said goodbye and walked away from her.

Chapter 5

After playing pickup at the neighborhood gym, KC, Taleed, and Chance met at DaRon's parents' home to play pool with DaRon's father. DaRon had not made it down to the game room yet. Due to out of town business, both Hakim and Chaz had been absent from this weekly bonding time for over a week.

DaRon soon made his way to the game room and greeted the fellows. When he stood by KC he said, "I went by one of my rentals in Greenbelt the other day, and this chick was there visiting my tenant. She was running her mouth about you. And I know it was you cause she mentioned the condo association where you live. What the hell happened between you and that Parker chick?"

"That girl showed up at my place. Then had the nerve to cuss me out. Man, I had to let that cannon loose. That broad freaked out after seeing a receipt for a ring I purchased for a friend."

"Whoa, whoa, a ring?" Taleed asked him.

"You bought some other girl a ring and didn't expect her to burst your chops?" DaRon said.

"Who's the girl?" Chance who had been flipping through the channels of the flat screen chimed in.

"Would y'all settle down? It's not like that." There was silence. KC looked around to find four pairs of eyes staring at him. "It was a ring I picked up for a friend."

"Spill it dude. You know it's more than just a friend." DaRon finally spoke his opinion knowing who would be the recipient of the ring.

"Okay, it's Shae. Remember she got all bent out of shape when I asked her to give me back my pinky ring. So I brought her one similar to it. It was only a small gift for a friend."

"Shae must be more than a friend to be on the receiving end of that kind of gift. When you give it to her, she's going to be at my house showing it off to my wife, you know that." DaRon told him.

"I already gave it to her."

KC was far from surprised by what DaRon said because of the close friendship MacKenzie and

44

Shaeterra shared. DaRon continued, "I can only guess at the small fortune you spent on that purchase."

"I ain't saying nothing else at this point," KC said and then sat facing the TV.

"You've said enough. Everything else we can pretty much speculate," Chance commented.

"Another wedding?" Taleed said.

"Who's getting married?" Pops joined the fellows in the game room.

"KC and Shae. He gave her a very expensive engagement ring," Taleed said.

KC turned, "You got that all twisted. Nobody said nothing about an engagement."

"I didn't even know the two of you got together," the elder Mitchell said to him.

"Pops, it's not the way this idiot here just explained. Yeah, me and Shae have been kinda seeing each other for about a month but it's nothing. The ring I gave her is basically a gift, something like a peace offering. I like her a lot—"

"We all knew Shae fell in love with you years ago when she—"

KC interrupted Chance, "Hey can we change the subject. So um, DaRon, when's the funeral?"

Pops placed the pool stick on the table and stared at DaRon. So did everyone else. When Nevada Majuava finally realized that DaRon, the man of her dreams, her college sweetheart, the man she wanted to be with, had gotten married, it didn't sit too well with her. She tried to ruin his wedding, but when that failed, she followed him around town. His routine was usually consistent but when he yelled at her at the gym it hurt badly and from then on out she cried almost every day over his absence.

After many phone calls trying to get him to speak to her, he gave in. The only day that he would meet with her, it didn't go as she had hoped. So on a busy street, Nevada committed suicide by standing in front of the vehicle driven by KC with DaRon as the passenger.

KC was able to stop the vehicle before impact, but another driver slammed into the rear of the car he was driving, which pinned Nevada between her vehicle and the one he and DaRon were in. After the accident, paramedics had to pry open his vehicle, but at least KC walked away uninjured. DaRon suffered a mild concussion and nearly lost his wife as well. Nevada was pronounced dead at the scene.

"Damn, KC. What a way to change the subject," Chance said to him.

Then DaRon spoke in a whisper, "Man I almost lost my wife because of what that girl did." Then annoyed, he glanced at his pops, "Even though we had history, I can't risk my marriage by speaking to her peps about when the funeral is going to be."

"I spoke to her dad." This time all eyes were on Chance. DaRon especially listened. He was puzzled as to why his best friend had not mention before today his conversation with Nevada's family. "My wife wanted to send the family some flowers and a sympathy card. You remember they were friends in college."

Joelee never knew the true relationship between DaRon and Nevada because he only admitted to her that Nevada was someone who "did" things for him, but after leaving school, both Joelee and Nevada promised to keep in touch and that's what they did. Nevada went to visit Joelee in New York for a weekend. They reserved a room at the Hilton in New York's Theatre District. Nevada wanted to see a Broadway show and do some shopping. They shopped and saw the play "Little Shop of Horrors" at the Virginia Theatre, and after the show, the two friends were given a backstage tour by one of the actors Joelle had met at a press party.

"How's Mac handling everything? Is she back home yet?" DaRon's father asked.

DaRon said, "She's fine; Jo brought her home last night."

"Yeah and if it weren't for Joelee, you'd be in divorce court. Mac was on her way to the airport. She was ready to leave your ass," said Chance.

"I know that and we talked about everything last night."

Then KC placed a hand on his cheek and asked DaRon, "You talk about that right hook of hers?"

Chance joked, "Damn! That was mean slap she laid across your face, dude. A Charlie Murphy slap on Rick James."

"She really feels bad about what happened that night. Oh and I forgot to tell you, she's coming over to talk to you," DaRon told KC.

"I'm going to need some back up when she gets here."

"Is that how you got that red mark on your cheek? What the hell happened?" Taleed inquired as he had not heard about the incident between the five friends.

Chance starting explaining what had transpired, "Mac was a little pissed off 'cause she thought DaRon's sidekick over here was the cause of him hooking up with Neva. Mac didn't know that I asked these two geniuses' to handle that issue they had with Neva. After we left the hospital, Mac wouldn't listen to me, nor my wife, but when KC here got the bright idea to stand in her way, pow! She slapped the living shit outta him. I'm telling you," Chance was laughing as he continued his story, "Google that video slap between Charlie Murphy on Rick James. That shit was mad hilarious."

There was laughter around the room, but as quickly as it started, it ended when a tiny voice at the top of the steps sounded.

"Hello?" It was MacKenzie.

"Hey, babe. C'mon down," DaRon said to her.

"Hey Chance, Taleed. Hey pops, how y'all doing?"

Buttercup was Chance's nickname for her. Pops waved and Taleed nodded up.

"KC, can you come up here for a minute, please?"

KC whispered, "Y'all got my back right?" Then he walked up the stairs to face MacKenzie who was smiling when he stood facing her.

She said, "Close the door." He did. "There's a whole bunch of feelings running through my mind right now and I'm not able to really come to grips with all that's been put in front of me. I'm having a really difficult time in my marriage right now because of what's happened. Confronting you is difficult, but I know I have to do this." With her head bent down she paused.

50

"Do you want me to tell you how I feel? You wanna know my involvement in all this?" KC thought that this would somehow ease her mind, but he was wrong.

"No, KC! I want you to listen to me. Please, let me tell you how I feel. I love my husband. I have for a very long time. Nothing, no one could have convinced me not to marry him. I expected that love in return, and from the day we said our vows I thought I had that in him. Because DaRon is so close to you, I don't know now what I have. And at the same time, I thought you disrespected our vows, stepped over the lines."

"Mac, I didn't," KC whispered.

"This girl tried to ruin my wedding! And to see you guys tearing up in the hospital without even telling me what had actually happened was the final straw."

After DaRon found out that Neva died in the accident, it changed his perspective and his behavior was noticeably different. MacKenzie picked up on it and searched the room of sad faces for answers. KC, Chance and Joelee were silent. Her own husband ignored her questions but confirmed what she knew with a tear that slid down the corner of his eye.

"I'm sorry but we all cut ties with her, Mac. We had to."

"But you went with him to see her. DaRon put that behind him after our marriage. He knows how much I value trust in our marriage. You took him to see his ex!"

"We went to apologize to her. I wanted Neva to know that I was sorry for being an ass to her. C'mon Mac. Chance told you this already. Don't torture yourself second doubting what you and DaRon have." Then KC closed the distance and wrapped his arms around her. "Give me a hug." She extended her arms and embraced him. They hugged as she rested her head on his chest.

When she pulled away she said, "I hated you KC. For the first time in my life, I hated you." Tears began to fall from her eyes when she spoke these words. "How could I hate you? I don't know, but I did." Then with the back of her hand she wiped the tears away. "But, you know I don't really hate you, KC. I love you, I do. I love you like the big brother you've been to me. I can't hate you, KC. I was only being emotional."

"I know that."

"What happened at my home a few nights ago was a mistake. I was angry because I thought everyone turned on me. Especially you, KC. I know how close you are to DaRon. Me and DaRon, well everything was great until I heard about him and that girl. I-I really am sorry for reacting the way I did." She reached up and touched the cheek that her hands once landed on a few nights ago.

KC thought that because they were all friends, he had to be the one to step up to stop her from leaving her husband who was not there to plead his case. They all knew DaRon did nothing wrong and KC wanted to let her know. But little did he know that someone so tiny could strike back so hard. And it hurt him.

"Mac, you don't have to apologize. I understand your feelings, hell we all do. We just hope that you and DaRon can work this out." He was sincere in the words he spoke. He also didn't want to get his face slapped again.

Chapter 6

Grandparents are typical. They discipline their own children, setting the strictest and most of the times unrealistic rules. But once their children have kids, they flip the script. Taleed's parents were no different. Every since they discovered they had a grandchild, the two of them spoiled him with gifts and toys. If you didn't know better, you would think his son was royalty. They spoiled his son and every other weekend when he spent time with them, his son had a new toy, coat, outfit or hat. His son even had his very own room in their home, the room Taleed once had as a child. Today when he picked up his son, Taleed noticed a new video game hooked up to his nineteen-inch flat screen that, by the way, his parents had purchased last week. What's so ironic is, as a kid, Taleed couldn't have a television in his bedroom. If in fact he wanted to watch TV, it had to be under close supervision and in the family room. It wasn't until he was a young teenager he was allowed his very own set in his bedroom.

Looking around the room, Taleed took note of the toy chest that was over flowing with stuffed animals, small cars and trucks, and Playschool toys. He'd never had this amount of toys growing up, and it pissed him off knowing his parents spent so much money on their grandchild and so little on their own son.

"Get your bag, boy," Taleed said as he snatched the video game from his small hands and tossed it on the bed.

Once he got to his vehicle, he secured his son inside of the car seat and sat behind the wheel. When he looked up towards the apartment where his childhood friend once lived, Taleed saw a half naked woman staring down at him. *Stupid ass chickenhead.* He said to himself. Adjusting the rear-view mirror Taleed asked his son, "What do ya wanna do now?"

"Umno." He shrugged.

"Well I do."

He drove over an hour through the suburbs and then through the busy city traffic. And once he pulled the sedan between her apartment and the abandoned buildings, he put the car in park and turned to look at his son. "Where are we?"

"Kena." Then he started giggling.

"Close enough." It was noon and he had three hours to spend with his son before returning him to his mother.

She opened the door to a smiling Taleed and his young son who stood slightly behind him holding onto Taleed's pant leg with one hand and the fingers of the other in his mouth.

"Hey there," she greeted him with a kiss, then bent down and said, "How's my big little man?"

"Boy get ya fingers out ya mouth!" Taleed scolded him and then walked inside the tiny apartment. "I have a few hours to kill before dropping him off to his mom."

"Ah. I missed you, little guy," she said while lifting him and kissing his forehead.

"Stop spoiling him, K. My parents do enough of that crap." He sat on the sofa, extending both arms on the back of it.

56

"What's wrong, Taleed?" Kendra asked as she sat next to him still holding his son. She didn't have any kids and had taken a strong liking to his son.

"Put him down." She did.

"What's wrong with you Taleed? You ain't never had a problem with me holding him before. Now it's a big deal."

"When I come see you, K, I expect you to show me some attention, not my son. You don't think I deserve some 'alone' time with you?"

"You jealous?" Taleed watched his son sit on the opposite side and then he laid his head on Kendra's lap. "Ah, baby, you jealous. There's enough of me for you and your son. Look at him."

"That's what I'm talking 'bout. He get enough attention from my parents and now you."

"He miss me, and I miss him too."

C'mere." Taleed stood and grabbed her hand. He paused so that she could remove his son's head from her lap. "Stay there and don't move!" he instructed his son.

"What?" Kendra was confused.

He didn't say anything, just led her to her bedroom.

"I want you to lay down with me for a minute." He pulled her onto the bed next to him and exhaled a long breath once she snuggled in the pit of his arm.

Kendra reminded him of a young girl who he befriended years ago because she had little direction in her young life. He thought back to a time she was out late with some older kids.

"What are you doing out here so late?"

"Minding my business."

"Get over here girl!" Taleed yelled. Three young men who were hanging on the stoop with her stood. Only one of the three Taleed recognized. Although he was only fourteen, Taleed was about to whoop his ass. The other teens had to be no older than sixteen. Gabbie walked over to were Taleed stood.

"Does your grandma know where you are?" He asked while reaching for her tiny arm. She lived in a one bedroom apartment with her grandmother who was being supported by the aide of the state. She was an unfortunate birth from a drug-addicted mother

and a street hustler now doing time in the state penitentiary. Taleed didn't want to watch her become a third-generation high school dropout because if she continued down the current path, that was sure to happen.

"She said I could stay out a little later tonight."

"I know she didn't say until midnight, and I know she don't know you're out here with knuclehead boys she don't even know. Get your butt in the house, now." She smacked her lips but followed his orders.

"She's only twelve, dude," he yelled at the trio.

"Man, what do you care?" the younger of the three snarled, turning his mouth up at him. Taleed walked within inches of him and towered over his small frame.

"Gabbie is my god sister," he said. "And I don't want you knuckleheads corrupting her. I know where you live, punk!" The teen blinked taking steps backwards. Taleed watched the three degenerates walk in the opposite direction.

Because of his encouragement, Gabbie finished high school and is now doing hair at a high-end salon.

Today, he snuggled next to a much older version of Gabbie. Taleed kissed the top of head and asked her, "What do you want?"

"Right now?" The question caught her by surprise, as she had never been asked such a serious question as this before. She certainly did not expect it from him.

"No. In life, K. What is it you want out of your life?"

"I guess I never gave it any thought. Eventually, I think I want to go back to school, get my GED and then take some college classes." Kendra dropped out of high school in the tenth grade because she had little ambition to finish. She, like most of the young kids in the neighborhood preferred to sit on the stoop late at night, party at clubs featuring the latest Go-Go band and sleep until past noon, just as their parents did in their youth. This behaviour, although not foreign to him, was not in his upbringing as Taleed's parents were strict and demanded that he focus on his education. His life was so different from hers and at times that bothered him.

"You need to start now. I don't want to see you like this. Stop letting your life waste away."

"It takes money to go back to school, and I don't have it. Look around, Taleed. Does it look like I'm loaded with money?"

"It also requires motivation and dedication, and if you're serious, I can help you get started."

"You will?" She looked up at him while still laying in the pit of his arm and when she did, he kissed her lips.

"Of course I will." The two lay quiet for a while, each absorbed in their own thoughts. Kendra didn't know what to make of Taleed's sudden interest in her life. He had never considered her finances before this day. Taleed pondered his future with someone who had very little drive. And if he kept her in his life she had to change. He intended to give her a start on completing her education.

He rolled on top of her and gently rested his body on each elbow. Playfully, he kissed her lips, then he pecked each cheek and stared at her. She is the only woman he's ever had any kind of feelings for, and at the moment he wasn't sure if those feelings were genuine enough for him to want more out of their relationship. He was indeed willing to give it a try.

He broke the silence, "I have to get my son back to his mom before she start blowing up my phone. Come walk me to the door." Taleed got up from the bed and walked out of the room. "Say goodbye to Miss Kendra," he said to his son before walking out into the hallway of the building.

Kendra hastily walked behind him. She had more to say, so before he could walk out of her apartment, she blurted it out, "I really miss you, Taleed." He gave her a whimsical look but chose not to respond because he didn't know how to respond. "Are you coming back?" Kendra asked him. She did not want him to leave. After her last boyfriend, he was the best thing to ever come into her life. Taleed was a much better person to her, unlike her former boyfriend who is now locked up on a misdemeanour. She longed for Taleed's presence and ached each time he was away from her. This time was no different. She wanted him to stay a little longer but Kendra understood his role as a parent.

Taleed looked at her as if he did not understand her question. Then he brushed a braid from her face and said, "I'll call you later." His son waved goodbye to her and followed Taleed down the stairs. Kendra stood at the door and watched until they were out of sight.

After securing his son inside the car seat, Taleed headed towards the suburbs to where Candice lived, thinking about his conversation with Kendra. *She might be the one.* That thought brought about a smile.

Looking in the rear view mirror, he asked his son, "You ready to see mommy?"

"Mommy," was his only reply.

When Taleed pulled the vehicle in front of the building, Candice and Woody were walking inside. He didn't give it much thought because the two of them had gotten close since Woody moved into the basement apartment. He did however wonder what they could possibly have in common. Woody was a forty-three year old divorcee with three teenage girls.

Chapter 7

After leaving the office, KC retrieved his cell phone and scrolled through the contact list for her name. They had dinner and drinks a week ago at Stan's, a popular bar situated across from the office.

"Deanna, my little chocolate drop," he said out loud while listening to the ringing phone. When she answered, she couldn't quite recognize his voice. It wasn't until he mentioned being with his friend did she remember the evening they had met. He bought her and her girl a drink when the two of them were at Stan's celebrating Deanna's new job promotion.

"How about we have dinner and maybe some drinks?" KC asked and then said, "I can pick you up if you'd like."

That wasn't necessary; Deanna lived within walking distance of the metro station and could easily take the train there and back. She was more independent than most of the women KC was used to dealing with. That was one quality he liked in her. Tonight he was hoping to find another quality to like about her.

When Deanna walked towards KC, to him she looked just as beautiful as she did that night he first laid eyes on her in Stan's. What caught his attention was her short, jet black hair, that deep bronze complexion, and full lips. Deanna was five-four and showed the right amount of cleavage. KC reflected back to that night. *That night I winked at the little chocolate drop to show my interest, and seconds later she and her friend was standing at my side.*

KC stood to greet her and then kissed her on the cheek.

"Glad you could make it, ma." Her jet black hair was slick close to her scalp and once she sat, KC couldn't help but notice those shapely legs and how that black v-neck dress she wore cling to her shapely figure. The night they met, he learned that she was a former dancer who now teaches it to teenagers at the metropolitan boys and girls club in southeast.

"I'm glad you called." Her smile was warm and sincere. KC motioned for the passing waitress.

"What would you like?" he asked his date. While buried in the menu, he caught a glimpse of her facial expression. Clearly it was him that she wanted.

But instead of being lewd, Deanna looked at him and said, "Merlot is fine."

They had dinner and drinks while engaging in some good conversation. But the one thing that didn't slip by KC was her sensuality as she flirted with him the entire time.

Deanna touched his hand and said, "I was supposed to hang out with my friend tonight. That is, until you called."

When the bill was placed on the table, KC reached for it, retrieved his credit card and slid it inside the plastic holder without taking his eyes off of her.

"Is this the friend who was with you when we first met?"

"Faye, she thinks I'm wasting my time meeting you here."

"Ah yeah. I remember that skank-ass attitude she had that night. It doesn't surprise me she would say something negative about me, probably about life in general."

"Why would you say that?"

The waitress retrieved the bill and said, "Be right back."

"As I remember, your girl had a foul mouth that night. Probably because my friend Chance didn't give her the attention I was giving you. And you had all of my attention, ma." He paused and then asked her, "So are you?"

"What? Wasting my time? I don't think so." She locked her fingers between his, "As a matter of fact, I know I'm not." She was flirtatious, just what KC was wishing for.

When the waitress returned with his credit card, KC signed the receipt and placed the card inside his pocket. He stood and then reached for her hand.

"Let's go."

"Where to?" she asked while he led her towards the door.

"Your choice. My place where we can have more wine and get to know each other on a more intimate level. Or I can take you to your place where we can say our goodbyes and I'll call you later for, hopefully date number three."

When they got to his car he opened the passenger's door and watched her slide inside. He got in and started the engine. As he backed out of the parking spot, she still had not answered. KC chose not to press her for one. He could easily drop off Deanna at her home and call up Jade, his standby.

"I like option number one better." KC smiled and steered his vehicle in the direction of his home.

Once KC got to the door of his condo, he opened it and Deanna walked inside. She took a quick look around.

"Relax. Make yourself at home," KC said after closing the door. He pointed towards the wine racks. "Take a look and see what you like."

Deanna turned to him thinking she had all she wanted standing in front of her. *Nice car, nice home, and good looking, too.* He was definitely a catch worth pursuing.

She retrieved a bottle of Riesling and handed it to him. KC popped the cork, retrieved two long stem glasses and poured their drinks. Before handing one to Deanna, he leaned in and placed a gentle kiss on her lips. Deanna smiled and reached for her drink. They both took a sip before KC placed his on the counter. He took her glass from her and placed it next to his.

Once again he took possession of her lips, then he leaned down to lift her frame by her bottom. KC wrapped both her legs around his waist and walked towards the bedroom. He crawled on the bed with her clinging onto him. Then he knelt over her and pulled her dress over her head. Deanna was completely nude. Her nipples stood at attention, waiting and ready for his tongue. KC reached for the left one and squeezed it while his tongue licked at the right one. Then he switched up; his tongue took possession of the left nipple while his thumb and forefinger toyed around with the right nipple. He heard her moans while she tugged at his trousers. KC stood and

70

removed them along with his shirt but froze, as he was mesmerized watching Deanna play with her shaved coochie. Then she reached for his member and guided it into her mouth. The feel of her moist and warm tongue broke him out of his trance-like state. Then it was his turn to moan his pleasure as her tongue licked the tip of him and her mouth sucked in as much of his meat as it could hold.

KC reached under the pillow where he kept protection and handed it to her. Then watched her as she ripped the corner of the package using her side teeth. She carefully removed the film and skillfully rolled it onto him. Deanna opened her shapely legs and spread her pussy lips wide open for him. Her pussy was about to get dicked down in a way she hadn't had before.

Thank you for slobbering on my dick but I will not be licking pussy tonight, KC thought to himself before he lifted her legs over both his shoulders, held on to her thighs and shoved his manhood inside of her moist, warm middle. He noticed her tightness, but that didn't stop him from repeatedly pounding his member inside of her pussy walls.

Deanna tried to reach for him but she was in an awkward position, so she simply held onto the sheets as she felt the shutters from her orgasms building. She wanted to switch positions but knew her partner wanted to be in control, and he did. Sweat dripped from his forehead onto her as he was on the verge of climaxing. Then KC heard her squeal in pleasure as he, too, finally gave in to his own orgasm.

With wobbly knees he released her legs, slowly withdrew from her and then collapsed on the bed next to her lifeless body.

After about five minutes, Deanna touched his shoulder and said, "You want something to drink?" He didn't answer. Then she picked up his shirt, pulled it over her head and walked out of the room. KC sat up, removed the condom and tossed it in the waste basket. He heard his cell phone vibrate. When he took it out of his pant pocket and looked at the display, it was a text message from his worst nightmare. It read: `Who is the bitch?`

Deanna returned with the drinks that he had poured earlier and handed a glass to him. He took a sip from his. Then his intercom sounded. Since he wasn't expecting anyone, he chose to ignore it. Deanna stared in confusion. When the buzzing stopped, his cell phone began vibrating. KC had a strong feeling that it was same person who had been hounding him for months now. He had to put an end to it.

"I can spend the night. We could cuddle," Deanna offered. She wanted to spend more time with her new lover in hopes of being in a serious relationship with him. She was tired of being the mistress, the side chick or the jump off. Deanna wanted her own man to love and come home to. But KC was deep in his own thoughts. He didn't want to cuddle nor did he want her to spend the night. His mind wasn't on her, nor Parker, Lucky, Jade or any other woman that he had in his bed. Lately, his mind was on Shaeterra.

"Some other time. I need to take you home." he said to her.

"Sure. Let me just get dressed." She reached for her dress and walked out of the room.

KC picked up the vibrating cell phone and said in a low solemn voice, "What is it?"

"How come you ain't answer the door, KC? You know it's me!" she screamed.

"That's why I didn't answer. Now stop following me and please stop calling me, Alex." Then he pressed the end button and at that very moment decided it was time for a new environment. KC got dressed and drove Deanna home. When he walked her to the front door, he placed a kiss on her cheek before leaving. Somewhere in the back of his mind he knew Alex was watching him. He didn't care.

Chapter 8

Chaz was sitting in his downtown office, staring out the window, daydreaming about the one woman who he said didn't deserve being in his future plans -- his model wife Chenia. Not after she abandoned him and their marriage—not to mention her only son. She was as selfish as a spoiled brat. Just recently, Jaxsen Morris was, for a short time, the center of his attention, but unfortunately it isn't her Chaz can't stop thinking about: it was Chenia, his former wife.

Chenia had to be in Anacortes, Washington for a Sunday morning photo shoot. His business associates were meeting with an important banker in Galveston Monday morning, Chaz had to be there for a mandatory meeting. Their late night candlelight dinner on the rear deck of his home was about the only time they could steal. When Chaz picked her up from the airport, they'd planned to spend the entire

weekend together—that is until she received the call to return to the West Coast. She hadn't bothered to unpack her luggage as given the limited time they would have together, there was no need. The bags remained at the entrance.

Her soft touch could be felt on his shoulder. Then her hands slid down the middle of his back. Chaz closed his eyes to savor the moment of her subtle passion. Chenia had an undeclared passion about her that would diminish any reservations regarding her devotion.

She laid the side of her head lightly on his back. "I don't want to leave you," she whispered while lightly stroking his arms. Chaz reached for her hand and at the same time stood, bringing her thin frame into his. Holding onto her, he knew it would once again be a farewell he didn't want. Their moments together seemed to be shorter than any previous visits. She had an extremely demanding schedule and Chaz had his equally demanding workload. Before this brief visit, it had been three weeks since they'd spent any time together. They would meet somewhere between her scheduled shoots and his board meetings. Chaz was dreading yet another extended and lonely three or more weeks without the woman who had captured his heart.

"Stay with me." Before she could answer, he captured her soft lips. She wrapped her arms around his neck as he lifted her. Hurriedly, Chaz walked with her in his arms up the spiral stairs all the while softly biting at her lips. She returned the passion.

Once inside the master bedroom, he deposited her body in the middle of the oversized bed. She watched as he began undressing her. When she was fully undressed, Chaz stood to admire her flawless body. She was simply beautiful.

It wasn't long before he straddled her and returned to consume her lips. This time their tongues found each other and established a sweet dance on their own. The two of them seemed to react to each other's needs as if programmed to do so. Without great thought, Chaz encapsulated both breasts within the palms of his hands, delicately holding each. Her nipples were hardened from the initial touch. She moaned in delight. So did Chaz once he started licking at each, one then the other.

77

"Chenia," he said before reaching for her face. She felt heavenly. A hint of lilac infused his senses. He then passionately kissed her mouth. She was receptive.

He felt her reach for the bottom of his sweater and began pulling it over his head as he stood. Swiftly, Chaz unbuttoned and removed his trousers before returning his attention back to her awaiting arms. She rubbed his freshly shaven head while staring into his eyes. The words she spoke confirmed what was already known: "I love you, baby."

"Damn! Why can't I stop thinking about her?" he said out loud.

"Glad to see you too." Chaz hadn't noticed that his friend and financial attorney, Maxwell Bradford was standing in the open door of his office.

"Sorry about that. Come in, Rocky." He stood to shake hands with his visitor. "I need a huge favor from you."

"Say the word." Maxwell sat facing Chaz.

"I need to refocus the structure of this particular company." Chaz continued to explain how with his financial background and those connected with his company, he could boost Keon-Chance Technologies to going public within the next three months. It was time his brother's company started trading publically. Both Chance and KC had been at this for a while and had encountered multiple roadblocks in doing so.

"Ever since my brother returned from working in the technology department in Leipeg Germany, he had so many brilliant ideas. Most were shelved."

"He's smart. Hell, I think he's a genius. And showed his uniqueness for talent when he sold his first idea to the military."

"Technology changes and is reinvented almost everyday. He has a knack for keeping in tune with high-end technology. That's what we as investors want to invest in."

"You're excluded."

"I know that, but my investment groups that I formulate for this purpose are not. Hear me out. His investment would have doubled, maybe tripled if Tech had chosen a different venue announcing their inventions. Projecting the future technology is an art, not science. My brother has a vision that extends beyond the next wave of inventions."

"That's an understatement."

"His latest quest is huge. I'm talking billions!"

"What's your concern?"

"Tech is a small company with high-end technology professionals, all of whom are on the edge of brilliance. As a financial investor, I have ideas that would make everyone at Tech and those involved very prosperous."

After listening to his idea, Maxwell asked, "Why me? You're his brother."

"And you're a friend. And as a friend, you should lead Tech through this venture. Trust me, I know what my gut is telling me. I've been at this for some time now. THG may have been a great idea in the beginning, but that route isn't working."

"Chaz, don't do this, man." Maxwell was sure that Chaz was bitter because of the breakup from Jaxsen. She led the effort of seeing the successful offering of KC Technologies.

"Do what?! What I'm doing is identifying a financial investment connection that Tech can build on."

"Don't take your anger that Jaxsen caused and turn it against her. You of all people know how to separate business from your personal life."

Chaz waved a hand in the air as if swatting at a gnat, "Somehow I feel that that ending between us couldn't be avoided. This has nothing to do with what happened between me and her. And besides THG would be right in the middle of the plan. What I'm proposing is for them to refocus. That's why you have to lead this effort because I can't be involved any further than the initial investors."

"Then, why now? If that wasn't your motivating factor, then why is it now you see a great financial investment opportunity for Tech?"

"Remember last month's conference in Vancouver? I managed to get a group of investors together who were jointly interested in giving up a lot of backing on a company. The deal fell through because of miscommunication. Tech can go public but in the interim they can be vested financially closer to home. I'm going on my gut instinct. I'm telling you Rocky, the money is there and this group is eager to invest in a sure thing and that sure thing is Keon-Chance Technologies." Chaz was sincere in what he was proposing to Maxwell who was cautious to jump the gun, but he'd known his friend for many years and there weren't too many occasions when his investment ideas went sour.

Chapter 9

Monday morning Chance and KC were deep in paperwork when Tricia came in and told them that Maxwell Bradford was on the line and wanted to speak to them both. They stared at each other and KC shrugged.

"Rocky?" Then Chance said to her, "Put him on speaker phone."

She did and left the room.

The three of them exchanged greetings before Maxwell summarized a financial plan that Chaz had put in place. Maxwell wanted the two of them to meet with him and his staff in his Georgetown office to go over it in detail. What he proposed sounded like an idea that would be beneficial to Keon-Chance Technologies and financially sound for the two owners.

After the meeting the two partners walked the block to have a late lunch in a small lounge located in the rear of the five-star hotel. It would be a welcomed change to eat at a decent time in lieu of shoving down cold sandwiches while working until midnight in the conference room.

Once entering the dimly-lit room, they were immediately surprised by the amount of women who sat around the room in groups of two and three. They were all wearing nice outfits as if going to a club. KC was pleased to have so many women to choose from.

"Good evening, gentlemen. How many will be joining you?" asked the perky hostess. She flashed a wide smile admiring them both; however, it was Chance she clearly was smitten with. "I like that tie." She slid her thumb and forefinger along the edge of his silk tie. The hostess was making every attempt to break the ice without blatantly crossing the line with harassment.

"Thank you," Chance said, being as polite as possible. He was clearly annoyed. "It's just the two of us for dinner."

"If I didn't have to work my shift, I'd love to join you." She waited for him to respond to her gesture. He stared expressionless. There was a long pause before she turned around. "Follow me please." Somewhere between their greeting and her flirtatious remark, the politeness in her voice faded. Judging by the grimace plastered on Chance's face, it's understandable why the change. He was irritated by her assertiveness, and it showed.

"Lighten up, Chance. She's only flirting. And it's not like you don't know what it's like to have females hit on you."

"I'm a married man."

"You weren't always. And as I remember, when you weren't married you were just as flirtatious with the honeys as she's being with you."

Their conversation continue and Chance said, "I never said I wasn't a lady's man with the honeys, what I'm saying now is, I'm no longer chasing skirt."

"All I know is there's too many fine looking women in this room to not chase skirt tonight."

"Now that, I noticed. I'm not chasing but clearly not naive to that fact." The two scanned the room but were interrupted by a soft voice.

"Me and my friend were wondering why two handsome men were sitting at this table all alone." Chance and KC both stared in the face of a very attractive woman before standing to greet the two of them.

"Hey, I'm KC and this is my business partner Chance." The two of them held hands with the two ladies as an exchange of greetings. "Ladies, have a seat."

"My name is Rochelle and this is my friend Teri," Rochelle spoke slowly in a southern drawl. She had a striking beauty that would cause any man to stare in awe. KC was no different. Chance tried his best to avoid making eye contact. She was slender, about five feet six inches, and very curvaceous. Her deep brown complexion was flawless. Her companion was slightly shorter. She was five feet, three maybe with honey brown skin tone. She was dressed plainly. Teri was as fascinated with Chance as the perky hostess, but judging by his aloofness, she too would get the cold shoulder. If he could have any woman in the room, she wouldn't make it on the list.

"What are you two ladies doing at the hotel?" asked KC.

"One of the local radio stations is sponsoring a jazz performance on the mezzanine level. It's usually a big event in town. Tonight we wanted to have dinner first. I take it that's not why you're here."

"We're in Georgetown to discuss an investment opportunity with an attorney next door."

"Really? That sounds interesting." Teri answered, sounding slightly keyed up, but soon returned her attention back to Chance. "How long are you gonna be here?" she asked gazing into his eyes.

"We're just having an early dinner," he responded in a monotone voice.

"But that doesn't mean we can't enjoy the presence of the two of you," KC chimed in.

"Where're you from?" But before either could answer, Teri noticed the silver wedding band on Chance's finger.

"I see you're married," she said.

"Yes I am."

"Would you excuse us?" Both Chance and KC stood and watched the two ladies walk out of the restaurant, probably in the direction of the rest room.

"Listen Chance," KC said quietly. "She may not be your type, but let's enjoy this while we can."

"You got that right. That chick is not my type. For all I care, you can take both of them gold diggers back to your house and do whatever."

"Hmm. That doesn't sound like a bad idea. I'm down for a little three-some."

"Did you see the sparkle in that girl's eye when you mentioned the investment meeting? Chill out with that until things are final."

"C'mon, Chance man, let's just have a little fun."

"I'd love to have a little fun tonight with my wife."

"Yeah well, don't ruin it for me because your ass is whooped."

"Not whooped. It's love. But you wouldn't know nothin' 'bout that."

Chance retrieved his cell phone and walked out of the restaurant.

After watching Chance walk away, KC took out his cell and stared at the display. He thought about calling Shaeterra but decided against it.

Chapter 10

After leaving Baltimore, the first place Taleed stopped before visiting his son was his girlfriend Kendra's apartment. When he wheeled the sedan in the alley on the side of her building, he retrieved his cell phone and dialed her number.

"Hey, babe," she greeted him when she opened the door. Kendra stood on her toes to reach him. He pecked her lips and walked inside her apartment. "Where you been?"

"Busy. What's up with you?" he asked.

"Nothing, just chilling. You want something to drink?" Taleed sat. He didn't want anything to drink nor did he have time for anything to eat. He came there for one purpose.

"Come here. You miss me?"

"I did, baby." She walked towards his outstretched arms and sat on his lap. He watched her as Kendra slid from his lap and knelt between his legs. Carefully, she unzipped his trousers and slid a hand inside, reaching for his manhood. After its release, she planted several kisses on the tip and then began licking the backside of it before inserting his enlarged member in her mouth. Taleed inhaled a long breath and rested his head on the back of the oversized chair. Kendra's tongue and mouth took over his manhood as she sucked and licked on him effortlessly. Slurping sounds were heard as spit dripped from her mouth onto his member. She stroked him with one hand all the while sucking on his member. Her head bobbed up and down as his moans became louder and louder. And when her mouth tightened and her rhythm slowed, Taleed could no longer sustain the pleasantry of her oral activity. He emitted a loud sound of pleasure and shot his load in the back of her mouth.

Kendra paused a moment and looked up at him before slowly removing her mouth from his now-flaccid manhood. She licked her lips and stood while Taleed adjusted himself. He stood next to her, exhaled a satisfied breath, rubbed his face with the palm of his hand and zipped up his trousers.

"Roy got out last week." Taleed paused. "He wants to come by and talk."

"Damn Kendra! Can I at least get my dick back in my pants before you hit me with some bullshit like that!"

"I just found out, Taleed."

"How? How did you know? Who told you he was out, K?"

"He called me. He called to see how I was doing"

"And?"

"I think," she paused and shifted her weight, "he wanna talk about our relationship. I owe him that, Taleed."

"The fuck?"

"I'm sorry Taleed, but that doesn't mean that I don't love you, because I do. I know that for sure. He just wants to talk, that's all."

"Look K, I don't know what your issue with this dude is, but he don't deserve you. Hell, he caused you to lose custody of your little niece! You do remember that, don't you?" Turning from her Taleed headed for the door.

"Don't leave, please." She reached for his arm.

"Don't touch me!" He pulled away from her grasp before turning around. "Tell me something." Leaning into her, he asked, "Who you gonna call when he starts putting his hands on you again? Huh?"

When Taleed first met Kendra, it was late one evening while he was listening to music while sitting in the van. Behind him loud voices were heard coming from a vacant lot. Two people were arguing, and a child was screaming at the top of her lungs. The man was short. He stood about 5'4", and was strong-arming the child while yelling profanity at the young woman who had a frightened look on her face.

In the hood these arguments happened all the time, so it wouldn't get most people's attention. People didn't care who could hear or see them. Being a father, Taleed was concerned for the child, but his cell phone vibrated, diverting his attention. When the call ended he looked back in the direction of the mayhem, the male was not there. He scanned the lot and the surrounding area. The young woman was cuddling the child and crying. Taleed exited the vehicle and approached the two. After introducing himself, he learned that Kendra Mathews and her boyfriend, Royce Walls were arguing over the child who was not hers but her niece that she had been giving legal guardianship.

Taleed saw an opportunity to turn a bad situation into something good. He asked, "Do you need a ride somewhere?"

"I live on the other side of town, Ames Place. He won't come back to get us." Kendra responded referring to her boyfriend Royce.

Reaching for her hand, Taleed opened the passenger's door. "Get in. I'll take you two home."

She was quiet the entire ride to the neighborhood she called home. The kid sat quietly in the rear seat, sucking on two middle fingers.

"Thank you. What do I owe you for the ride home?" she asked as she prepared to exit the vehicle.

"You can do something about your situation," he told her.

"Why do you think I want to? He's not like this all the time."

"Let me call you."

"He got my cell phone."

"Get it back from him, and I'll call you."

He handed her a piece of paper, and she scribbled something.

Taleed watched her walk up to the dark building, and then looked down at the note. A slight smile spread across his face after reading her message.

"We're just gonna talk, Taleed, that's it, just talk."

"Yeah right. You tell me what you think I want to hear just so you can treat me like a sucker? Don't you know me by now? I'm with you because I like you K, and I see some things in you, in us, in-in our future together, so I thought."

"But, Taleed--

"Fuck off."

"I need you, Taleed." Just then his cell phone vibrated. But he pressed the side button ignoring it.

"For what, K?" he took his cell phone out of his pocket and looked at the display. It was a text message from Candice. "What do you need me for? To keep him from kicking your ass? K, if that's what you want to go back to then it's not me you need. You need help."

Tears swelled in her eyes. Taleed lowered his tone, "We talked about you going back to school to get away from this situation. We talked about it because I care about you, K. I care."

"I know, Taleed."

"You gotta put an end to what y'all had, K. I want you to forget about that sorry ass muthafucka, but if you don't, you can lose my number. I'm not shitt'n with you either. You can't have both of us. And I'm not gonna be played either." Taleed walked out of her apartment and stared in the face of an angry man who stood at least six inches shorter than Taleed's six foot frame. Judging by the man's body language, he was willing to take on a challenge. Taleed too was ready and prepared to knuckle up if he had to.

Taleed's first reaction came without much thought. The .45 was neatly tucked away in the glove compartment inside the car. *Damit*! He cursed to himself. He had not come prepared for trouble. Not the kind of trouble he knew Royce was associated with.

"Roy, what are you doing here?" Kendra asked him after stepping from behind Taleed.

Roy continued to stare, so did Taleed who took a defensive stance.

Then Taleed said to him, "Yo man, no disrespect but your girl chose. I'm that dude and I ain't looking for no bullshit from you and no interference in what me and K are building here. But know that she chose. *I'm* with her now. And if you don't like it, then I'mma see to it that you gon' have a serious problem with me. I don't know you like that and you don't know me like that. So let's keep it that way."

"Yeah, whatever!" Royce said to him under his breath. Before leaving he gave Taleed one last stare then turned and walked away not expecting confrontation from another man. He had been in Kendra's life for the past three years, however; didn't think she had enough backbone in her to let another man come between them while he was doing time. That answers his question as to why she never accepted any of his calls while he was locked away.

Taleed watched Royce walk down the stairs and out of the apartment building. He turned to Kendra and with the back of his hand, slowly slid it down her cheek.

"You with me now, right?"

She nodded. He kissed her cheek.

"We goin' look into other places for you to live cause I don't want you here anymore where dude think he can just show up when he want to. I don't want that, you feel me?" Again she nodded. He turned and walked down the stairs and out of the building.

Chapter 11

Chaz and Maxwell were in Chaz's downtown office reviewing some legal forms. Because he had been attending a speaking engagement in Toronto, Chaz had been unavailable to his attorney to go over the forms that would release his company from any dealings with the investors he initially gathered for a different offering.

"Everything looks really good. I mean with your brother's company," Maxwell informed him.

"That's good to hear. You know I meant to call him last night when I got to BWI. We still on target?"

"As far as I know we're going to make the deadline. Tech was scheduled to meet with THG this morning, and I'm meeting the group this afternoon to listen to their pitch. Chaz, I'm sure everything will be fine."

"That's good, man. That's real good."

Meanwhile, in the outer office, Gennie, Chaz's assistant, was responding to emails at her workstation. Unexpectantly, Chance walked in and greeted her.

"Hey, girl. How's it going?"

"Chance." She smiled at him. Gennie liked her boss's younger brother. What woman in her right mind wouldn't. He was strikingly handsome. But she respected him too much, and besides, she liked her job a whole lot better.

"Is my brother in?" Chance asked and she nodded.

"He's with Rocky, but you can go in." He thanked her and then walked inside his brother's office.

"Speaking of the devil." Chaz stood to greet and to shake hands with his brother, so did Maxwell. "What are you doing on this side of town?"

"We had a brief with THG this morning. Just thought I'd stop by. When did you get in?"

"Last night. Late."

"I'm really impressed with the progress of the IPO so far. It's going smoother than I expected. And thanks to you guys, we were able to scrap this dog and pony show. And with everything going on with my wife, I really need to spend more time with her. You know, be the family man."

"Thank your brother. He pulled this together," Maxwell stated.

"No doubt, bro, that goes without saying."

"I'll let you two get back to business. I'm out." Chance said,

"Hold on, I'll walk out with you." Maxwell turned to Chaz and asked, "We all clear?"

"Actually, I need to discuss another issue with you before you leave. That's if you don't mind."

Maxwell sat. "Not at all."

When the doors to elevator one closed with Chance riding down the eight flights to the garage, the doors to elevator number two opened on the eighth floor. Jaxsen Morris exited and walked directly to Chaz's office. Gennie stood and said, "Ms. Morris." But judging by her determined walk, Jaxsen was not about to be stopped. Gennie sensed this and decided not to try and stop her.

"So we're at war now? What kind of game are you playing, Chaz?" she huffed out of breath. Jaxsen knew she was wrong for coming to the office and barging in on him, especially because he was in the middle of a business meeting with his attorney. This was unlike her and she was aware of it, but there was nothing she could do about her actions. Her feelings were hurt and she was beyond being out of control.

Surprised by the sudden outburst, both Chaz and Maxwell turned towards the commotion. Then Chaz looked from her to Maxwell. *What the fuck?* is what Chaz thought. But then he calmly said to Maxwell, "Can we please have a moment of privacy?" Maxwell stood and walked out.

"Please sit down so we can discuss whatever this is." Chaz pointed to the chair Maxwell had just vacated.

"No! You're trying to muscle me out of this contract THG has with Tech."

"Absolutely not. This is a business decision that's best for the success of—"

"You-you, you're trying to get back at me for ending this-this thing – whatever we were having."

104

"Well it was an abrupt end to what I thought was a beautiful connection that me and you had. But it was more than just a 'thing' as you call it. This new direction is not about you and me, Jax." Then he whispered and said, "Have a seat. Let me explain my vision."

"Don't you dare," Jaxsen was seething. Don't you dare patronize me."

"Please have a —

"Bullshit!" He watched her stomp her feet like a child having a temper tantrum. Chaz had never witnessed this kind of behavior from her in this way and it surprised him that she would carry on in this manner. She was aware that her tone carried throughout the office and others could hear her outrage.

"Jax," he calmly spoke her name hoping it would settle her raging attitude.

"You low down—"

He interrupted. "Jax —

"Dirty son-of-a—"

Jaxsen!" Chaz didn't give her a chance to further humiliate him.

"I see what you're doing."

"If you'd give me a chance to explain, you'd understand THG is very much a part of this deal. I haven't excluded you or the company—"

"Then why am I being reassigned if it has nothing to do with me!?" For six long months she had worked with both Chance and KC trying to move their company forward. Now that she's no longer a part of this campaign, Jaxsen felt betrayed, not only by THG but by the three men.

"I-I don't have an—"

"Oh, go fuck yourself, Chaz!" Jaxsen turned and stormed out just as abruptly as she came in. A part of him wanted to run after her, comfort her, bring her feisty behind back in his office, lock the door and make passionate love to her. Then the other half couldn't muster the courage because his heart still had not mended by her sudden dismissal of his feelings.

Maxwell returned.

"I see that didn't go so well."

Chaz stared at the opened door. Her final words stung and he was crushed by them. He felt he did everything to try to win her love. He thought he was the perfect gentleman; took her on romantic dinners, showered her with expensive gifts, and most of all, spoiled her with his passion. So far, he seems to be striking out in the love department. First Chenia leaves him for her modeling career, and now Jaxsen leaves but without any real explanation. Maybe it was time for him to throw in the towel. The good thing about his life at this point was his son and not to mention, the redirection of Keon-Chance Technologies. With the vast amount of filings, presentations, speaking engagements and meetings they had lined up over the next three months, it would surely keep his mind occupied. It had to. He could not allow this failed relationship with Jaxsen to destroy what he was working so hard to achieve.

Chapter 12

Today was the only day in a long time that Taleed had to himself and he wanted to spend it with his son. So he called his son's mother to invite them out for a day at Rollie Pollies. Candice needed a break, and besides, he knew she would enjoy seeing their son have fun at the kiddie gym, that's why he included her, and it was a good decision to do so.

For the first time in the months after her move to Maryland she seemed happier than he's ever seen her before today. She was almost giddy. Her jubilant behavior made a favorable impact on his son's sprits as well. He ran around the game room for hours before Taleed grabbed him away from the jungle gym for a bite to eat.

All that running around was tiring. When Taleed looked at Candice, he saw that she was exhausted as well. She had given up running around the huge play room chasing after their child. Taleed decided it was time to wrap things up and leave.

When they got to the car, Taleed strapped his son inside the car seat. Candice sat in the passenger's seat and leaned her head against the headrest. After he started the car, Candice turned towards him and smiled. She said, "Thanks for inviting me." Taleed turned around and noticed his son's head was bent forward. He was out cold.

"You had fun, huh?"

"Yeah. I did. I really did." That was about the extent of their conversation during the half hour ride back to her place. When he parked on the side street, he got out and unstrapped his son. Candice had already made it to the door and held it open as Taleed carried his son inside and into his bedroom.

"You can stay if you want." Candice stood in the hallway outside his room. She didn't think anything of her offer. He is the father of her child. She didn't care if he slept on the couch or in her bed with her. Candice wanted companionship with someone other than Nicolas. It wasn't the same. Candice didn't feel the same way about Nicolas as she felt for Taleed.

110

Maybe it was because they have a child together, but for some reason she had stronger feelings for him than she did for Nicolas. She would never tell him, but the more they spent time as a family, the more he was growing on her.

Her invitation caught him off guard making Taleed stop from what he was doing, preparing his son for bed. He stood up and looked at her with a curious expression. *Wow! Do I really want to stay?* He asked himself. Then regained his composure and pulled the comforter over his son's small frame. *Yeah, but am I tired or horney?* His thoughts were on overdrive. Taleed stood and reached inside his pant pocket for his vibrating cell phone. Looking at the display, he thought of her. *Damn.* He did want to end the evening with Kendra.

Still speechless, Taleed cleared his throat before saying, "The last time I stayed, things got a wee bit out of hand, don't you think so? I ain't making that mistake again." That was the night Quintin got caught by the jump out boys doing a drug deal down on Monroe. Previously, Taleed had warned his friend that they were going to catch up to him eventually, and they did.

He had just walked in Candice's apartment to get his son when the call came through from Quintin's girl Malleo. So he left and when Taleed got to the police station, they had already taken Quintin to lockup. Malleo was hysterical. Her sister Travia wasn't much help either. That girl was all over him from the moment Taleed sat between the two of them, consoling Malleo and trying to calm her nerves while Travia had a firm grip on his dick. Every time that girl was anywhere near Taleed she'd find a way to brush up against him. Taleed's probably the only dude on the East side of Baltimore that has never had her in bed, and he'd plan to keep it that way. There was something foul about Travia and Taleed didn't trust her.

But somehow that night, Taleed managed to pull away from her grip and when he did, he dropped the sisters at their home and drove back to College Park to be near his son. Exhausted and horny as hell, it was nearly two in the morning when he crashed on Candice's couch. He didn't know how he ended up in her bedroom on top of her, fucking her like he straight out owned her pussy.

Taleed chuckled and then said with a smile, "We already resolved that issue so I'll pass."

"I was only asking because it's been a long day for all of us, geesh." Taleed walked to her and bent his head lower to meet her stare. She didn't budge. The way he was feeling now would not be fair to Candice. Sometimes when he's around her, these weird feelings surfaced. He could feel his dick. This night was no different from any other night that he'd been around her. Even though Taleed was horny and it wasn't a secret, he wanted some ass tonight. But it wasn't right to be thinking this way about her. Candice was different from Kendra; Candice was weak and Taleed knew he could take advantage of that fact but it would backfire, and he knew it. He had to ensure her stability for the sake of his son. Besides, Taleed wanted to try to at least build a stronger relationship with Kendra. His son liked her a lot and that mattered a great deal to him. Since his son was asleep in the next room, Taleed wasn't about to bend his mother over and punish that thang cause judging by the look on her face, Candice was practically begging to get dicked downed.

"Yeah, it has been a long day. That's why I'm driving back to B'more." Candice blinked away any thoughts she previously had and then Taleed asked her, "Not that I really care but what would your boyfriend think if he knew we fucked?"

"Is that what you call it?" Then she turned up her nose and thought, *That is so foul for him to say that to me.* Candice hated that he didn't feel the same way about being physical with her that evening as she felt. They had sex, made love, Candice couldn't understand why he just wouldn't admit to it.

"It is what it is," he joked.

"Maybe I just don't want you to leave, Taleed." That didn't come out the way she intended it to so she tried to correct herself. "I mean... maybe we can talk."

Once again he stared at the face of his cell phone. This time, instead of a missed call, it was a text message from Kendra that simply read:

`Miss U.`

It wasn't the text message that caused Taleed's head to spin nor was it what Candice just said. It was

114

the way she said it. Her tone was different now, and he didn't know what to make of it. Taleed was almost afraid to raise his head and when he did, her eyes had a trance-like grip on his.

"Are you late for something?" she asked, noticing his constant glances towards his cell phone and now his blank stare.

"What do you want?" This time he was going to force her to tell him what her intentions were. He was either going to spend the night with her in her bed or leave now to go be with Kendra for the rest of the evening. But Candice said nothing. She stood there staring at the floor. This frustrated him even more. Without another word, Taleed placed the cell phone back inside his pocket and walked towards the door.

"Taleed wait—"

"Ain't got time for this bullshit," he said as he walked out into the common area.

Taleed heard her say, "Then go." Just as he slammed the door.

Chapter 13

Papers were scattered throughout the mahogany conference table. Maxwell was at the white board with a marker in hand while Chance stood at his side explaining the current state of the company to the group of investors. Although each represented different companies, they all sat on the same side of the table. The group had been at this session for four hours straight, and except for the one ten-minute break, they were fixated in this fifteen by fifteen glass enclosure. Roger, Keon-Chance Technologies' financial advisor, sat in the corner of the conference room intently staring at the figures presented by THG. Harper, the lead representative from THG along with his five-man team and KC all sat on the same side of the table. KC looked at the clock and then over at Tricia who was busy taking notes and capturing the black marks being scribbled on the whiteboard. Soon it would be time for KC to take over the whiteboard and plot out Tech's initial response to what the THG team presented. He stared at his notes and waited for Maxwell to end his speech before looking down at his vibrating cell phone. It was an incoming text. KC did not want any further distractions, so without looking at the display, he turned it off.

After addressing the proposed plan THG so carefully laid out during nearly six months of being the lead on this venture, the group ended the meeting promising to reconvene with just the management staff in the morning. Chance and KC stayed a little longer to wrap up some loose ends with Maxwell and Harper.

Harper explained to both Chance and KC what to expect from the agencies. The two listened intently.

Then Maxwell added, "Let me be honest with you guys, everything you do is going to go under a microscope. Your character is going to play an important part in whether this deal is successful or whether it fails. That not only goes for you two but you need to convey this to Tricia and everyone on your payroll." He added, "Everyone!"

After about an hour, the two of them left. Tricia peeped her head inside the conference room.

"Hey, if you guys no longer need me, I'm leaving now."

"We'll see you in the morning." KC said.

Chance turned towards her and asked, "Do you have a ride home?"

"My boyfriend's downstairs. Thanks for asking. See you guys in the morning."

"Hey, you want to get a drink at Stan's?" KC asked Chance after Tricia left.

"Actually, I'm going home to have dinner with my wife. I've had enough of this place." He stood and said, "Why don't you have dinner with us."

KC thought about it for a minute then said, "I think I'll pass." He walked out behind Chance.

Once they got to the front office, KC reached for the receptionist's receiver and dialed a number.

"Later man," Chance said as he nodded up at him and walked out of the office.

He returned the nod and said into the receiver, "Hey lady," when she answered. "Wanna have dinner with me tonight?" He waited for a reply before saying, "Where you at?" Shaeterra had not left work so KC drove down Wisconsin Avenue to get to the building where she worked. Because of the limited parking in Georgetown, he was hoping she would be waiting outside and she was when he pulled up to the curb.

"Can we go to JPs?" she asked after sitting inside the vehicle.

"What? No Sequoia's?" KC asked because he knew that it was her favorite seafood restaurant that was only a block away on the Potomac.

"Boring." She simulated a yawn and lightly patted her mouth. "Tonight is live jazz night at JPs." She beamed.

"Tonight? Live jazz on a Wednesday night, sweetie?"

"Yeah. They're under new management. When's the last time you were there?"

"Obviously not for a while. I guess it's JPs." Instead of having dinner in the city, KC drove to JPs located in the suburban area.

During dinner, they listened to the local jazz band play remixes from various artists and talked

120

mostly about her family because he knew very little about her. Only the fact that she grew up with Mac, DaRon's wife. Shaeterra was the youngest with two much older sisters, raised in Lanham where her parents remained.

After dinner, the two shared dessert which is something KC would never do. He was not much into dessert. He would rather have Jack on the rocks. Maybe it was being in good company but for some reason he especially enjoyed her conversation. Her laughter at his jokes was sincere, her smile genuine. He wasn't ready for the evening to end, but KC was tired and needed to get her home because of the early appointment with Harper and the rest of the THG team.

"As much as I hate to, I'll take you home," KC said after the server returned with his credit card and receipt.

"Why do you say it that way?" Shaeterra asked innocently. KC smiled and looked at her, knowing that she was just as naïve as he originally thought when they first met in his friend's basement. She was just as naïve when he invited her to his home and tried unsuccessfully to make out with her.

"No reason at all," he said but thought, *If I wasn't as tired as I am, I'd take you home and lock you up for a night of unbridled passion.*

Their conversation continued during the short ride to her home. When he pulled into the parking lot and turned off the ignition, she said, "This is the first time I've been with you and you haven't checked your phone messages."

"That's because I didn't want any interruptions." He swiped the tip of her nose with a finger. Shaeterra smiled before KC leaned in and kissed her on the cheek. He waited by the entrance and watched in admiration as she walked inside the apartment. "So you're not going to invite me in?"

Shaeterra looked at him with a slight grin and said, "Goodnight, KC."

Why am I doing this? He asked himself.

When he got back inside the vehicle, he turned on his cell phone. Immediately it began vibrating, and as he started the engine, he watched the counter display two, three, four, five unopened text messages

122

and seven voice mail messages. *This chick is crazy!* He said aloud. *Alex will not let this shit go*!

Before pulling out of the parking spot, he looked at the first text from her. It was an irate message threatening him once again. He pressed the delete button without looking at the other four. He began planning how and what to do about her constant harassing phone calls and uninvited visits. KC dialed DaRon's number.

"Can you meet me at JPs? I have something I need to talk to you about." In less than ten minutes he was sitting at the bar discussing alternative living arrangements with the one real estate agent that he could trust and knew could make moves fast.

"Dude, I wish you had said something to me earlier. I had a vacant room in College Park that I just rented a few days ago to this cat that's going through a divorce. I know it wouldn't be permanent for you but at least it would be a quick escape."

"Damn! I just thought that bitch would go away."

"I got some things lined up. Let me get back to you." The two friends touched fists before DaRon left the bar.

While sipping on his drink, KC retrieved his cell phone and dialed a number. Without waiting for a greeting KC said, "Yo, Imma need a huge favor."

Chapter 14

DaRon had enough information to assist his friend in acquiring a new place of residence. Getting out of PG County might be a good start. KC stayed at the bar to have a second drink. His phone vibrated just as he ended the call with Taleed. He looked at the display. It read: Felicia. The name didn't register but because the number was in his contact list, he answered.

The sultry voice said, "What's going on, handsome?" KC didn't recognize the voice. "You forget about me already, poppi?" Slowly the tone was becoming clearer. KC loved the slight accent from her. It reminded him of someone he had lusted after for so many years, the now deceased Nevada Majuava.

"Felicia. Where you been hiding, ma?"

"I've been patiently waiting on your call."

"Is that right?" He was dragging the conversation. "So when can I see you again?"

"Look up, poppi." He paused and scanned the bar. Then he grabbed his drink, stood and walked on the opposite side of it were she sat still holding her cell phone to her ear.

"Do you mind if I sit?"

"Please."

"What're you doin' sitting here all alone?"

"Well, I was supposed to meet my girl, but she called after I got here and said she couldn't make it. I figure, why not have a drink. Then when I spotted you, I knew I made a wise decision."

"Hmm. Yeah you did. Looking just as good as the last time I saw you." KC gave her a once over. She had on a mini skirt that attached itself to her toned thighs and a black laced corset. "Is that outfit legal?"

She smiled while KC continued to stare in hopes a getting a glimpse of at least one of her nipples. Half her breasts were already exposed. KC took a sip from his glass and peeped once again. He had to come up with a line to get her out of the bar and into his bed.

But he had to wait for the opportunity to present itself.

Felicia knew he was a player. She saw him leave with Shaeterra the night they first met at JPs. She really enjoyed dancing with him for nearly the entire night, but she had come there with friends. KC was fine as hell. She still wanted him; she was just not going to chase after him. If KC wanted her like she did him, he'd have to make the first move. But he didn't even call and now, two months after their first meeting, here he is. This must be her lucky day.

"You wanna buy me a drink?" she asked. He grinned. *That was too easy.* He thought.

"What are you drinking?"

"Chardonnay."

"Ya know I have that same brand at my house." She smiled.

"Cute, KC."

"So are you, Felicia." He winked at her and said, "You can leave your car. I'll bring you back." KC stood from his seat and reached for her hand. She took hold of it, turned the stool towards him and stood. Felicia tugged the hem of her skirt as it had

127

risen up her thigh. The two of them were unaware that every man around them, including the bartender had their eyes glued on her backside. And when KC ushered her towards the door, he took the opportunity to get a quick look at her rear end also.

KC unlocked and then opened the door to his condo. He watched her as she sashayed inside. Then he looked towards the ceiling and mouthed a quiet, *Thank-you.*

"Relax, ma. Look around if you'd like. The kitchen's to the left, the bedroom's on the right. Take a pick."

"How about that glass of wine you promised."

"Then follow me." He retrieved an unopened bottle of Chardonnay from the refrigerator, placed two glasses on the counter and filled the two glasses half way. Felicia grabbed a glass and took a seat at the bar, KC followed. "How is it?"

"Nice."

KC placed his drink on the bar and turned to her. She turned her stool to face him. "You're looking real sexy, ma." Then he placed one hand between her legs and the other on the side and began rubbing it. "You feel good, too." The more strokes he applied to her leg the closer his hand was getting to touching her middle. She was not wearing panties. Once he made contact with the crease of her pussy lips, she softly moaned and he used the other hand to pull her face towards his lips.

KC stood, still massaging her middle and holding her in a lip lock. She wrapped her arms around him. He released her lips, lifted her from the bar stool and planted her feet on the floor. Then he removed his shirt.

It was now Felicia's turn to gawk at him. He was definitely eye candy. She reached for his pectorals and did not see KC reach inside his trousers for a small plastic wrapper. He removed his trousers and turned her around to face the counter. KC tore into the wrapper and shielded himself. Then he pulled up Felicia's skirt and pushed her forward, forcing her to bend forward and balance herself on the counter top. Slowly, he slid his member inside her moist middle and then slid both hands inside her top, locating her nipples. She moaned as he pumped himself in and out of her middle and squirmed beneath him when he simultaneously squeezed both nipples. He released them and grabbed her by her hips and lifted her petite frame from the floor. She held onto the counter for support as KC was ramming himself into her and at the same time pulling her hips into him.

"Oh, Oh, Oh," she managed as her orgasm was rising to another level. His manhood and being in this position touched that spot. KC was giving her the wood like no other man had done before.

KC knew he would hit her erogenous zone in this position. Beads of sweat dripped from his forehead onto her backside as he continued his thrusting and pounding into her middle. Her moans became louder and then he felt the walls of her pussy lips vibrate, sucking on his manhood. She let out a loud sound of pleasure. His breathing became heavier as he felt his own orgasm escape.

When he was finished, KC planted soft kisses on the back of her neck, withdrew from her middle and lowered her body back to the floor. Felicia noticed the hand prints on her hips but it didn't matter, she was a satisfied woman.

"Where's the bathroom?" she asked while lowering her skirt. KC pointed behind him, then picked up his trousers. Felicia walked towards the rear. KC walked in the kitchen. He used a paper towel to remove the film from his manhood and then slipped into his trousers. He was completely dressed when Felicia joined him in the living room.

"I'll take you to your car," he said flatly. He had yet to fully recover from the workout session they'd just had.

It was a quiet ride back to JPs. KC wanted nothing more to do but sleep, but he promised to take Felicia back to her car.

When they arrived at the nearly vacant lot, he said, "Call you later."

Felicia didn't like the sound of that because it usually means another two months, if that at all. She tossed him a smile and leaned towards him for a kiss. KC didn't move nor did he move away. He simply lowered his head to meet hers and puckered his lips.

Chapter 15

Candice stood by the opened door with Lil' Man standing by her side. He had been crying. "What's wrong with you, boy?" Taleed bent to kiss the top of his head. Then noticed a pink overnight bag in the corner of the room.

"He's punished for misbehaving at day care. Tell Daddy what you did," she said and then closed the door.

"What'd you do, boy?" Taleed asked him but he simply lowered his head and said nothing. Taleed figured he would have a talk with him later. He also could tell Candice was a little bit fed up because she huffed and walked away. He followed her into the kitchen and so did his son.

"Going somewhere?" he asked while taking a seat. Instantly, his son crawled in his lap.

"Yep. Before I start work on Tuesday I'm gonna visit my parents for the weekend."

"And Nicolas," he added sarcastically.

"He's still my friend whether you like it or not." To her his sarcasm sounded like he was jealous. Secretly, she hoped he was jealous that she was spending time with another man. If she couldn't get Taleed to pay attention to her wants, maybe this would give him a kick.

"Whatever, man! You need a ride somewhere?"

"Nope. Woody said he didn't mind taking me to the metro. I'm sure he would take me to Union Station if I'd asked him to." Two weeks ago, DaRon had rented the bottom unit to an older man who went through a rough divorce and needed someplace in a hurry. He wouldn't have rented the unit to just anyone because of the fact that there were two single females in the building.

DaRon was extremely careful about whom he rented his multi-family units to, and he had several. So he asked Taleed to run a background check and to find out as much information on the man that he could find. This was the one assignment Taleed didn't mind doing because if Woody was going to be living this close to his son, he wanted to make sure the man wasn't a pedophile. But everything checked out fine. It turned out that after meeting Woody, Taleed actually liked the guy. Candice did as well because he was helpful to her. There was nothing about him that gave either DaRon or Taleed cause to be concerned.

"That's cool. Hit me up when you get there," Taleed said and then placed his son on the floor. "Go give mommy a kiss and let's go."

The next day, Taleed drove to his parent's home for a visit. They loved having him bring their grandson over for a visit. When he got out of the car and walked to the rear to get his son out of the car seat, some neighborhood kids who had been riding their bikes came over to the car.

One of them said to him, "Taleed, who kid is that?"

"My son."

"Your son? Where have you been hiding him?"

Taleed placed his son on the pavement. "Have you done your homework, boy?"

"I did some of it?"

"How is that every time I ask you that question you got the same answer? Go back inside and do the rest of it."

"Does he live with you, Taleed?" the young lad asked before Taleed closed the passenger door.

"My son lives with his mother most of the time. Now if that answers your question, take your butt back inside and finish your homework."

"Hello there, Taleed." He looked up to see the young lad's mother standing in the doorway of the apartment building. She was dressed in a tattered robe and had pink foam rollers in her hair.

"Malleo, you need to make sure that boy finishes his homework before he comes outside. What's wrong with you?"

"What's wrong with you not coming over to see a sista like you used to?"

"Don't get it twisted. I was doing my boy a favor. That favor didn't involve servicing you. You need to worry about being a mother to little shorty and stop trying to get yo freak on all the time." After his friend Quintin got locked up, Malleo went and got herself knocked up by a cross-town rival gang

136

member. She was close to delivering. Malleo never made the smartest decisions in her life, getting pregnant again was probably the worst. Taleed wanted to make sure Quintin's daughter Kimmi wasn't planted in the middle of any turf disputes.

"You need to stop kidding yourself, Taleed. Everybody know you want this."

"Yeah, along with them nasty pink hair rollers, the dirty house shoes are a deal-breaker. You need to put some clothes on." He took hold of his son and walked towards the home of his parents. "And put a paper bag over that head." He mumbled to himself while walking inside the house.

Chapter 16

Joelee pulled her vehicle in front of DaRon's home. She knew he was out looking at some property but MacKenzie was there. When she walked in the two of them hugged each other.

"I'm sorry I haven't been by before today," Joelee said.

"Don't worry about it."

"Is everything okay? I mean with you and DaRon."

"Some days it is. Other days, Joelee, I want to break his frigging neck. But I love him. That I know for sure.

They walked inside the family room where both Trinidad, Chaz's son, and Taleed Jr. were playing. Joelee said, "Hey there Taleed. How are you?"

"Fine." Is all he managed to say. Joelee smiled after receiving a tiny hug from Trinidad.

"How did you get to be the baby sitter?"

"Taleed's parents are away on vacation and this little guys' mother went to North Carolina. Me and DaRon like having him here with us and Tri likes it too when he comes over. I tell you girl, having these two here has helped me through these tough times. I can't tell you how many times I wanted to just walk out and leave this all behind me."

"His mother lives in North Carolina?"

"No, she lives in the College Park now. DaRon rented one of his multi-family homes to her. She might be visiting relatives or friends down south."

"You look so much like your father." Joelee said while lightly tugging at his wild hair. Similar, but much tamer than his father's twisted locks.

"And nothing like his mother."

"You know her?"

"Never met her. That kid has Taleed Wallace written all over his face. Seems impossible to carry a child for nine months and have him look nothing like you."

"That is unbelievable. Who is his mother?" Joelee was curious.

"Your guess is as good as mine. Taleed doesn't talk about her and neither does anyone else. I don't know why."

"I wonder why."

"From what I gathered, something happened surrounding her pregnancy that caused a whole lot of tension between some of the brothers, especially DaRon and Taleed. I only got bits and pieces in small details. They're the only ones that know what happened."

"From what little I heard from Chance, I got the impression that Taleed has an excessive dislike for her."

Taleed and DaRon met while attending the university. Instantly, they became friends and they pledged the same frat. Soon DaRon introduced him to the rest of the fellows. He was also close to Joelee and Candice. Joelee was like a baby sister to DaRon and Candice was Joelee's friend from back home. DaRon knew that Taleed and Candice fooled around their last year in school, but it hurt him to the core when he found out that Taleed had gotten Candice pregnant.

"That's an understatement. But he's not exactly easy to get along with either. The way I look at it is, what happens between them, stays that way. Even though I don't like it when they hold something from me, like my husband seeing another woman."

"It's not that way Mac. Don't' think like that. He was protecting you."

"Yeah. I'm slowly coming to grips with that, Jo. Still don't like it though."

"I'm curious why they want to hide it, the mother of his child, I mean."

"Don't be. I wasn't privy to much because of being on the West Coast. As I understand it, everything started sometime around the end of his senior year at the University. You should know more about that than me. You guys went to school together."

Joelee was confused. She tried to think back to their days at the university. Then she started counting the years.

You guys went to school together... You guys went to school together... You guys went to school together...

Joelee thought about what Mac had said and thought back to the year she graduated.

DaRon took her to the ESPN Zone to celebrate. It was crowded that evening. DaRon wanted to celebrate her graduation away from the festive activities at the university. Joelee didn't care what he had planned as long as it was off campus. Without transportation, she rarely left the campus. After four years of living in a seven by twelve room, she wanted freedom. After being seated, everyone engaged in conversation with whomever was seated the closest.

She watched Hakim make small talk with KC, then listened to Neva speak to DaRon using some Spanish words and at the same time noticed Candice and Taleed heavy in conversation. This especially caught her attention because the two of them were snuggling up with each other in an unusual manner. Joelee had never seen Candice act this way towards any man on campus.

"I had fun last week." Candice was always more straight forward in conversation than Joelee, especially when it came to the boys in school. At times her personality would be interpreted as overtly flirtatious. Joelee, on the other hand, was raised by two church-going southerners. They were two narrow-minded individuals whose entire existence revolved around religion. Candice's parents were more liberal.

"I'll bet you did, sexy," Joelee heard Taleed say. "When are you leaving town?" She watched him reach for her hand.

"Sunday. Anything going on tonight?" Candice asked him.

"I wouldn't know," he responded.

"You can make something happen, Taleed."

"That's not my thing, at least not consistently."

"Do you want to get into something before I leave town?" Candice asked him.

"We'll see about that," he whispered realizing that Joelee had been listening to his conversation.

"If not, can we at least exchange phone numbers?" Candice asked him.

But then Joelee's attention turned to KC who was finishing his drink. He stood.

"Leaving so soon?" DaRon asked. And almost instantly, it was if the clouds covered a sunny ski. What Joelee remembered, after being overjoyed all day with graduation activities, is being overwhelmed with sadness after hearing the two of them exchange conversation about the man she fell head over heels in love with four years before this day. The man she shared her first kiss with. The man of her dreams, her first love, now her husband.

Joelee shook her head and repeated out loud, "We went to school together..." while staring at the toddler trying to form a combination of her childhood and college friend Candice's likeness to that of the young Taleed. There were none.

"Joelee? What's the matter, Joelee?" MacKenzie asked with concern in her voice. Joelee wondered if their relationship created an offspring? *Could this child be the result of their hidden relationship?* Once again, she started counting the years and added them to his age. Joelee shook the thoughts from her head, but in the back of mind, knew it was possible.

"Why so many secrets, Mac?"

MacKenzie rolled her eyes upward, "Back in the day, when they were in school, there was no breaking that unity between them. I've seen it my entire life. But you know what, after what happened when DaRon was in the hospital, things between me and him will have to change. That is, if he plan on making this marriage work. I'm his wife and as his wife, he should trust me and not keep secrets. Like you and Chance, you guys share everything because he trusts you."

Chapter 17

Baltimore is truly a beautiful city but as with most inner-city neighborhoods, there were neglected districts the city government basically turned its back on. The streets were lined with potholes, sidewalks were cracked and weren't well paved, the play areas had outdated gym equipment and the common areas didn't get much attention from the parks department. Taleed's family wasn't poor and they could afford to move to a better neighborhood, but this was home. He grew up in this town and so did his parents.

After high school, some of his friends chose to stay close to home. There were several well-known colleges located within minutes of each other. Taleed chose a college two hours away and stayed on campus for four years. He felt that in order for him to grow up and out of his friend's shadow, he needed the space.

He liked his neighborhood and made it his business to keep some of the kids that he sometimes referred to as knuckleheads in line. Some if not all of the young children, preteens and teenagers looked up to him because no matter how long he was away from the neighborhood, he'd always come back to check on them.

He had come home for a holiday weekend and noticed a few of the neighborhood kids playing in the common play area. Kimmi, his friend Quintin's daughter was only three years old when her father went to jail on possession charges. Her mom Malleo did a poor job of raising her. Thankfully, Quintin's half-brother Gavin was still in her life. Now she's eleven and just as fast as her mother. Her playmates, a few preteens, were roughhousing. One of them had an aluminum bat and was vandalizing what was left of the playground equipment.

"Hey!" he yelled at the kids. "Why y'all wanna tear up er'thing?"

"It's a piece of shit, anyway."

"Boy, watch your mouth. Who taught you that word?"

"What word? Shit? Everybody say it, it ain't no big deal."

"Just cause er'body say it don't mean you have to use foul language. How old are you now, pipsqueak?"

"Eight. Old enough to take care of me," the youngster said with pride.

"Yeah, right. You can barely talk. Have you finished your homework yet?"

"Huh?" he looked confused.

"Did I stutter? Have you done your homework?"

"I don't have to do no homework."

"That alone says you don't know how to take care of yourself."

"You ain't my daddy." He smacked his lips. Taleed grew up with this kid's father who unfortunately is now serving time on possession charges.

"If I was your daddy, your ass'll be flat on your back with that foul mouth. Why don't you go inside and do your homework. When you finish, I might be nice enough to show you this new PS2 game I picked up."

"Is that what you got in that bag?" The kid reached for the bag but Taleed snatched it up and away from his grasp.

"Not telling."

"Oh c'mon Taleed, you got a new game?"

"Go inside and do your homework. Don't come back out until you're done. I mean it."

"Man, how come I can't see it now?"

"Beat it, Shorty, or imma give you something to whine about. That goes for you too, Kimmi. I don't want to see neither one of you guys in this playground area until you show me your homework, neat and completed," he said while watching the two of them scurry inside the apartment building. Taleed walked in the opposite direction to his parent's home. Before going inside, his cell phone vibrated. Taleed stopped by the entrance and said, "Whaddup?"

It was KC on the other end. Taleed had promised to take care of a little problem that had been plaguing KC for too long. He had a plan, just had to wait for the right moment.

"Trust me dude, I'll let you know when er'thing is done."

Chapter 18

KC and Chance were at Little Rock National airport waiting for the return flight to BWI after meeting with two of their investors. Harper and his team had taken an earlier flight. KC and Chance had wrapped up the final presentation at the hotel conference room an hour ago. Chance was on the phone with his wife. The only person KC thought about the entire time was not Deanna, whom he hadn't seen or spoken to since the night of their workout session in his home, but Shaeterra. He retrieved his cell phone from his pocket and dialed her number.

After their initial greeting, she asked him, "Are you home yet?" Shaeterra sounded excited. It was three weeks since the two of them last spoke.

"We're at the airport in Little Rock waiting for our flight."

"You sound tired."

"Long day and a long trip."

"Ahhhh, I miss you." KC placed his head in his free hand and exhaled sharply. *I needed to hear that.*

"I'll call you later," he said before ending the call. KC sensed Chance staring in his direction. "What?" he said to his friend.

"Man, do you know this is the last trip we're going to be taking for Tech," he said. KC gave him a weak smile.

"The last one? You mean no more BWI? No more National? Can't wait to get home. And how come we got this layover anyway?" KC complained.

"'Cause your ass wanted to sleep in. Nobody told you to shut the fuckin' bar down last night."

"Yo dude, that bartender was fine as hell. You saw the way she was looking at me. If I wasn't so drunk I would've taken her back to my room."

"Yeah right, so what's up with you and your girl?"

KC smacked his lips and said, "I don't fuck with Parker no more. She's demanding not to mention how selfish her black—"

"Man, please. I'm glad to hear all that and what not but that chick was not your type in the first place. I was talking about Shae."

"Like you never wasted your time on some chick before."

"Oh yeah, we played the honeys back in the day. We were young. But I got over that shit quick. When I went to Germany after graduation, I learned so much man. Not just about technology, but I'm talking about culture as well. When I came back, I wanted more, you should, too. Tell me you don't. Not once did you pick up the phone to call anyone until now. Stop wasting your time with tired useless booty." He paused to listen for the flight announcement. "I heard that conversation between you and Shae. Three weeks is a long time to be away from your woman. She's the one you miss being with. I miss the hell out of my wife. That's why I call her when I can."

"I dunno 'bout Shae. I need to have a talk with her when I get back home. The thing is, I feel something for her, I do. I don't know what it is though."

"Yeah you do. She's the only woman who you haven't bent over."

They exchanged stares before KC changed the subject. "So how is Jo? I hear she and Mac are getting closer."

"Which is a good thing. Joelee keeps her focused about seriously working on her marriage. Mac was going to walk out on DaRon and leave his ass high and dry. And I think if he fuck up with the slightest thing, she'll claw his eyes out."

"Have dinner with me. I'll pick you up in fifteen minutes." KC was already walking out of the door of the condo. He drove through the city to the apartment she shared with two other women.

Shaeterra wasn't ready when she opened the door to the apartment, so KC took a seat in the living room. There was no television to watch or music to listen to, but there was entertainment provided by her roommate Julie who strolled through on her way to the kitchen dressed only in pink lingerie. His eyes followed her knowing this display was intentional because she'd flirted with him on several occasions before in the club. Julie twirled around showing off her thong and when she opened the refrigerator she bent over making sure KC had a clear view of her round ass.

Shaeterra must have some psychic powers because she came out of her room in stealth mode and scolded her roommate for prancing around the apartment half nude. Julie didn't care. She continued sucking and smacking her lips on the lollipop while strolling back to her side of the apartment.

"I'm ready." KC stood and followed her out.

"Nice outfit," KC said when they got to his vehicle. He opened the door and waited while she slid in the seat.

Shae was wearing slim fitted slacks that fit her small frame well and a matching short top with a thick elastic waistband and puffy short sleeves-- cool and fitting attire on a sweltering August evening.

"How did everything go?" she asked once they were seated in the restaurant.

"Flights were delayed. Equipment was lost. What ever could go wrong went wrong the entire time we were in that hick town. As brutal as it was, I didn't invite you out to talk about Tech's road show."

KC was surprised when after dinner, she agreed to come back to his place. Shaeterra too didn't want their date to end so soon. Once they were inside his condo, KC walked in the kitchen and poured her a glass of wine and turned on the CD player. Soft jazz bellowed through the speakers. He sat next to her on the couch while she sipped her drink.

"Shae." He used the back of my hand to stroke her face. "Tell me what you want from me."

"Would it surprise you if I told you I'm not as clear of my needs tonight as I've been in the past?"

"Why is that? What changed since I left?"

"You haven't called in weeks, KC. The time away from you let me reassess my feelings and what I want in the future."

"You said earlier when I called that you missed me. Please explain that to me. Tell me what you missed." She was quiet and chose to stare off into space. KC stood bringing her small frame into him. They exchanged looks moments before he held her tightly in his arms. Her body molded into his. She

155

was warm. "Shae," KC whispered her name. "Tell me you want me." KC waited for her to answer and when she said nothing he stood and asked her, "Are you ready to go home now?"

He walked Shaeterra to the door of the apartment and waited for her to enter. Before doing so she turned to him.

"Thanks for dinner." She did want him but not in the same way he wanted her. Shaeterra didn't want to be in a relationship with a man without any kind of commitment. KC had too many women in and out of his life and Shaeterra didn't want to be number three or four or five.

Chapter 19

When his cell phone vibrated, Chance looked at the display. It was an unrecognized two oh two number. "This is Chance," he said.

"Yeah, it's Rocky. I need to talk to you. Can you come to my office?"

"What's up?"

"It's about your partner. Something has come to my attention and I need to speak to you without him a.s.a.p. When can you get here?"

Chance looked at his watch, removed the cell phone away from this ear and stared at it before saying, "I'll be there in an hour." Then he pressed the end button on his cell phone and placed it in his front pocket.

He then yelled, "KC! Hold down the fort. Gotta run out for a few."

Chance hated navigating through the mid-day traffic in the city, but Maxwell's request seemed urgent. He parked in an underground garage one block from the building. Once he walked inside the Georgetown office, Maxwell was waiting in the reception area. The expression on his face spoke volumes; this was not going to be a friendly meeting. The two exchanged greetings, and then Chance was ushered inside of Maxwell's private office where plaques and certificates lined the walls. Photos of his friends and family were on display on the credenza that sat in the corner of the spacious room. One in particular caught his attention--a framed picture of Maxwell holding a certificate standing next to his brother who had an arm around his shoulder. Both Chaz and Maxwell were friends throughout under grad and grad school.

"Have a seat." With a stern look, Maxwell pointed to the chair facing his desk and walked around it to sit.

"What's this all about, Rocky?" Chance was concerned.

"Chance, when we started on this path to going public with Keon-Chance Technologies, several important facts were explained to both you and your

158

partner. I specifically told you that Keon-Chance Technologies and everyone involved in the company were going to be under a microscope. Your company's business ethics, financial records as well as your and your employees' ethics are scrutinized during this process. That includes you, KC, Tricia, and those database guys you have on payroll. Obviously, KC thinks this is a fucking joke, and I don't appreciate his attitude, nor do I care very much for his behavior." He leaned forward and said, "You're wasting my time –

"Whoa, whoa, slow down. That's my boy you're talking about."

"Well your boy is about to cause your company to be denied its IP by running around chasing skirt. Man, he's picking up chicks at bars. He-he got women stalking him. Like, two women hating on his ass and possibly a third. That's because he's disrespecting them. That shit don't look good at all. Damn! How much ass does he need in a week's time? His action raises a red flag with the commissioner and that's not good for your company. This shit ain't good for mine either."

"Damn! I knew about some of this, but I didn't give what he was doing on his own time a second thought. Let me talk to him."

"No. Absolutely not! This is beyond talking, Chance. We're too far invested in this already. Your brother put his ass on the line to make sure this deal works out in your favor. If this offer is rejected by the commissioner, we're talking about millions down the drain. And we didn't come this far to let that happen. Let me make a suggestion."

"I'm listening."

"If you want to continue, and I believe you do, you'll take my advice. Take it for what it is, but I suggest you remove him from Keon-Chance Technologies and disassociate yourself with him. Keon is setting a bad example for the company."

"What? Man, you're asking me to give up a twenty-year friendship."

"Yes. For two, maybe three, months." Maxwell paused and then said, "If you want to be in the game with the big boys, you've got to play the game with the big boys. I don't care what you do after we go public with Keon-Chance Technologies, but during

160

this process you have to let him go. This is not only your reputation on the line, it's mine and your brother's and I know damn well I'm not going to let this shit fuck me over because of some over zealous sex drive 'your boy' has. Believe that!"

So many emotions ran through his mind while navigating through the busy city traffic. *This had to be the worst fucking day of my life.* Chance thought. How could he part ways with his business partner and one of his closest friends? They had been together long before middle school. KC had been there when he needed him. He was there with him the day Chaz told him about the death of their parents. KC was by his side when he decided to quit school and play hooky. That didn't last but a day because when the school administrators called Chaz to inform him of Chance's absence, his brother had little pity for the grief that he was enduring, nor did he spare KC from a butt whooping. Not the kind of butt whooping you get from a parent but the beating you get from a sibling that included punching, choking and whacking up side the head. He was no match for his bigger brother.

Chance loved his brother for the discipline he received. He needed it and because of it, he stayed on the right path in life. He stayed focused. That's the person he needed to talk to about this dilemma.

Chaz had been in Springfield, Ohio for a three-day conference. This was the second day, and he was about to resume another meeting when his cell phone vibrated. He looked at the display before accepting the call from his brother.

"What's up, man? I'm about to go into a meeting so talk fast."

"Hey, I didn't mean to bother you. Can you give me a call when you're free?"

Chaz stopped walking and stood next to the entrance of the conference room. The tone in his brother's voice caused him to pause.

"I got a minute. What's going on?"

He listened to Chance explain the meeting he had earlier with Maxwell and how he suggested removing his closest friend from the company that he started, but together, the two of them built. And like so many times when Chance was young and even as a young adult Chaz gave him the advice that he knew his brother may not want to hear but needed to be said. He explained how the situation could go wrong on so many levels and his options if that were to occur. Chaz also proposed the positive side of this separation and how Chance needed to handle the departure in a delicate manner to prevent involvement from the attorneys of Keon-Chance Technologies and those his friend would hire to represent his interest.

"KC is a smart man, he's a business man, but most of all, he's your friend of twenty-plus years. Don't let the friendship get in the way of business, and Chance, don't let the business relationship end your friendship. Let me know how it goes."

By the time the conversation ended, Chance knew the position he was going to take with KC. They had been friends since a very early age and he didn't see exchanging words with him. But in the back of his mind Chance knew how volatile his friend was given the amount of personal stress he had endured in the past few weeks. This situation had to be handled delicately.

Chapter 20

Taleed was at the rear of the car securing his son in the car seat when he heard a tiny voice call his name. "Taleed." He turned to look and see who it was. "Where're you going now?" She was the spitting image of her father, Taleed's childhood friend. Seeing her reminded Taleed of the last time he saw his friend.

It was an early autumn morning, and Taleed was leaving home to make his eight o'clock class. Because he didn't live too far from the university, and like many other residents, he spent his weekends at home. It was only a two-hour drive. As he drove his vehicle out of the community his old childhood friend walked towards the car. At this time in the morning, the only people that pounded the streets were vagrants, school children, and your common neighborhood hustlers. Quintin was a well-known drug dealer on this side of town. He chose this path after the tragic death of his father and his mother abandoned the family after giving birth to his younger sister. That's when his half-brother Gavin came in to help him learn the game. Hustling, in his mind was the only source of surviving and supporting the two of them. Now he had an infant daughter to take care of because he screwed the neighborhood hoe and got her knocked up. He was only nineteen, three months younger than Taleed, and just like Taleed, too young for fatherhood. Being someone's parent was the furthest thing on his mind. Taleed had warned Quintin on many occasions to leave Malleo alone. She and her sister were "triffl'n hoes," as he put it. On this morning, Taleed didn't have time to talk to him because if he had stopped to talk, it would have made him late for class. That was the last time he saw Quintin. Word on the streets is Quintin got picked up by the police on possession charges only hours after Taleed pulled away.

"I'm going to take care of grown up business. Why do you ask?" After four years of seeing Kimmi playing in the neighborhood playground, the only change was her height. She was skinny, five four and almost ten. She was still and acted like a spoiled child.

"I want you to do me a big favor."

"What?" he eyed her cautiously wondering what tale her mother had been drilling her with.

"Take me to see my dad."

"Now you know I can't do that." Her father was arrested nearly ten years ago. They were old friends, but even Taleed wouldn't go and see him. Malleo had asked him on numerous occasions to take her to see him, and now she was using her daughter to do the begging. Quintin was going to be away for a long time, and because they found an unregistered weapon on him that was associated with several unsolved murders, additional years were added to his original sentence.

"Why not?" she pouted, folding both arms across her chest.

"Kimmi, your daddy is not exactly staying at the Hilton Hotel. He wouldn't want you to come to a place as cold as where he is. Besides, if your grandmother ever found out that I took you there, she'd kick my behind. Is that what you want?"

166

Kimmi's grandmother on her mother's side was mean as a junk yard dog. No one in the neighborhood ever crossed her and if they did, they wouldn't live to see another day.

"I just want to see my dad, Taleed."

"Oh, now you don't care about me," he joked.

"Taleed, please. I don't even remember him and mommy don't have any pictures to show me what he looked like."

"I'll make you a promise." There was one promise Taleed made and that is to never step one foot inside a prison no matter who got locked up. And Taleed was not about to be on the wrong end of the law, close but never crossing the line.

She beamed. "Yeah?"

He peeped in the rear passenger window to make sure his son was okay. Little Taleed had fallen fast asleep.

"If you do good in school, I'm talking about A's and B's, no C's, when school let's out this summer, I'll take you to see him. How does that sound. And this stays between you and me."

"Is that a promise?"

"Yep. Pinky promise." He extended his pinky finger to her and the two locked pinkies. Now go inside because I don't want to see you hanging outside after dark."

Taleed watched her walk inside, and when she did, he slid inside the driver's seat and drove out of the city. Before he could get on the Baltimore beltway, his cell phone vibrated.

"What is it, Candice?" He listened in irritation to her questioning him about when he would be there with their son. I'm on my way," Taleed told her, knowing it was far from the truth. He had one more stop to make before heading that way.

Two hours later he was walking inside Candice's apartment. This time, she was not happy to see him.

"You said you were on your way, Taleed."

"He's here, aiight?" he answered.

"No, it's not alright. I have to feed him, bathe him, and get him ready for his bedtime. Your job's done. You just drop him off and go be Columbo in some dark alley or something."

"I'll do it." Taleed walked towards the bathroom.

168

"What? What are you doing?"

"I'll bathe him," Taleed said then asked his son, "Whada ya wanna eat?"

"Hotdog."

After running lukewarm bath water for his son, Taleed walked to the small kitchen and retrieved a pot. Candice ignored him and went to her bedroom. After bathing his son Taleed watched as he chewed on his hotdog. He looked at his vibrating cell phone and smiled. It had been two days since his last visit.

"Hey, babe, what's up?" It was Kendra. She usually called about this time knowing if he wasn't working a case, he would be on his way to Baltimore. When he told her where he was, she invited him over. But before he could answer, he noticed Candice standing to his side. He stood and then said, "Let me hit you back." He ended the call.

"That was rude," Candice said a bit upset that Kendra had the nerve to call him while he was there.

"No, what was rude is you tryna listen to my conversation. C'mon L'il man, time for bed." Taleed cupped the top of his son's head and guided him towards his bedroom. After kissing his son goodnight, he returned to where Candice was standing. She had not moved.

He asked, "What's it to you who I'm talking to?"

"It's rude of her to call while you're spending time with your son."

"I'm usually not here at this time. She had no way of knowing—

"You didn't have to answer the call, Taleed."

"Damn, Candice. How would you feel if I didn't answer your phone calls?"

"Like you haven't?" There were a few times when in fact Taleed had sent her calls to voice mail, but that was only because he was in meetings or on stakeout.

"Yo! What's your problem? I gave him a bath, I fed him and I just put him to bed like I said I would and you still salty." *Sick of this chick playin'g stupid ass games*. Taleed thought to himself as he started for the door.

"Is that where you going now?"

He stopped before reaching the door and in an exasperated voice said, "I'm going to see someone who respects my privacy." Then he asked, "Do you need anything else?"

Those were the last words she wanted to hear, but Candice said nothing nor did she stop him from leaving. She was helpless as she watched him exit her apartment without saying another word to her. She stood by the door and wondered if things with Kendra were getting serious. Why wouldn't it? Candice had fallen hard for him when they were in college, which is why it was so easy for her to give into his advances.

Chapter 21

Early Friday morning, Taleed received a call from Candice asking him to take their son for his weekend visit with his grandparents sooner than he normally would. She had plans to visit family and friends in North Carolina. He wasn't too happy having to cut short his plans to satisfy her, but nonetheless he didn't argue. It usually fell on deaf ears.

He reached for his keys from the nightstand and stood.

"Hey." Rarely did he spend the night but whenever he did, it made Kendra happy to have him in her bed. "What time is it?"

"A little after seven."

"Where're you goin' so early?" Kendra asked as she rolled over and watched him. She was still sleepy. "I was going to cook us breakfast."

"Some other time. I have to pick up my son." He bent down to kiss her cheek. "Call ya later."

As soon as he entered her apartment, Taleed said to Candice, "I see you and your punk-ass boyfriend getting close."

"I'm going to see my mom and dad." Which was far from being true. Her parents were away on vacation, but he didn't need to know the real reason why she was making this trip to North Carolina; it had nothing to do with her seeing Nicolas.

"Sure you are. Is Woody taking you to Union station?"

"Get your bag." She told her son, ignoring Taleed who stared at her backside. She turned and handed him their son's jacket. What Taleed didn't know is that Candice sensed his eyes glued on her backside, but she didn't say anything. She was flattered. If going to North Carolina was getting his attention, she was going to do it every weekend. "I'll be back Sunday, probably around noon."

He left the apartment and drove to his parent's home. Taleed had work to do and didn't have the time to watch his son for the entire day. Besides, Taleed's parents loved the idea of having their only grandchild visit with them.

That Sunday afternoon, Taleed tried to reach Candice but his calls went directly to voice mail. Later that night, he went to her apartment, but she wasn't there nor did she call Woody who was waiting to pick her up from Union Station.

It was Tuesday morning and Taleed still had not heard from Candice, so he called Woody once more. *Where you at girl?* He asked himself. After speaking to Woody, Taleed decided that he would drive down south hoping to talk to her parents and find out where Candice was holed up. First, he had to take his son to DaRon's house. Taleed didn't want to take his son with him; this trip might not be an ideal trip for his son to come on.

DaRon greeted Taleed at the front door and noticed he had his son standing by his side.

"Can I talk to you for a minute?" Taleed looked at MacKenzie, hoping she would give them some privacy. She stood. "Lil' Man, go with auntie Mac."

"Come on big guy. Let's get something to snack on. How about a fruit roll up?" she said to him while walking hand in hand towards the rear of the home.

"I need a favor." DaRon shrugged his shoulder as if beckoning him to ask. "His mom left town last Friday. She was supposed to come back like two days ago." Taleed was concerned. "I've been calling but she not answering her cell."

"Did you try her parents?" DaRon was becoming concerned as well. He cared for Candice also.

"Yeah. No answer from them either. I left a few messages at her parents and on Candice's cell phone for her to call me back. Woody, that dude you rented the downstairs unit to, was supposed to pick her up from Union Station, and he said she hadn't called."

"That's not good."

"Naw. I hope she aiight."

"Look at you. Ahh, you care about her." DaRon teased him.

"Of course I do, man. She is my son's mom, ya know. I still gotta make sure she aiight and all. Ya know for my Lil' Man." That was his excuse. Taleed was concerned that something bad had happened to Candice.

"That's the complete opposite of the way you treated her when he was first born."

"Things change, man. You wanna drive down with me or what? I hate taking that drive at night through those back-end winding roads." Then he added, "But I don't wanna take my son. He'll just get in the way.

"That's not a problem. Mac would love to keep him." DaRon was concerned because if something happened to Candice and if her boyfriend Nicolas had anything to do with it, he knew Taleed would do something he'll regret. He wanted to prevent his hot-tempered friend from getting into trouble.

The two friends took off heading south in search of Taleed's son's mother. Instead of driving his tinted-out gas-guzzling sedan, Taleed took the first shift driving DaRon's even larger gas guzzling SUV.

Once DaRon pulled into the street where Candice's parents lived, Taleed instructed him to keep driving.

"Make a u-turn and kill the lights," Taleed said as they sat and watched the house. He was in his element, watching people without being seen. There was a light illuminating from the upstairs. A television was on at the bottom level, and when a small frame walked past the upstairs window, Taleed said, "I know this chick is not in there...Let's go." Then exited the vehicle.

He rang the doorbell and waited. No answer. He ranged it again and then loudly knocked on the wooden barrier. Still no answer. They stared at each other. When Taleed turned the knob, they heard a small voice.

"Who is it?"

"Who the fuck you think! Open the door, Candice!" Taleed yelled then turned to DaRon and said, "I oughta kick her ass." There was some shuffling and then the door locks released. Candice walked away not even bothering to make eye contact with the two who entered.

"I was going to call you back—

"But you didn't. You were s'posed to come back Sunday!" She was disheveled. Her hair was out of

177

place, she wore an old, slightly torn sweater, a dingy t-shirt and oversized jeans that slouched below her waist. Taleed knew something was wrong.

"What happened to you?" he asked her. She lowered her head to avoid making eye contact. "Candice!" Taleed lifted her chin. Her face was stained with dried tears. She had been crying. "What happened?"

"Nothing, Taleed."

"Don't tell me nothin'. Why are you crying?" She looked at DaRon who stood to Taleed's side. He too had a concerned look on his face. Taleed turned to him in hopes of getting some assistance from his friend.

"Candice," DaRon's voice spoke with compassion. "When're you going to realize that he care 'bout you. I care about you. If something is wrong, talk to him. I can leave you two alone if that's what you want."

"It was a misunderstanding," she said before turning away from Taleed. He reached for her arm. She grimaced and at the same time pulled away. There was a bruise on her shoulder only noticeable after the sweater she wore slid down one arm. Taleed cautiously stared at her before speaking. DaRon's eyes were beaming down on him. This didn't look too good to either of them.

"A misunderstanding between who?" DaRon asked.

"Just a friend. Like I said, it was a mis—"

"Cut this shit out, damn it!" Taleed yelled, now obviously fuming at Candice for avoiding his questions.

"I don't want to talk about this."

"That's too fuckin' bad 'cause I'm asking. And you gonna tell me the truth. Is this so called friend of yours as beat up as you are?" Taleed asked while removing the sweater she wore. She tried to pull away from his grasp but failed. Both arms had fresh bruises. "Who did this shit to you?" He pulled her shoulder length hair away from her face. There were hand prints around her tiny neck. It was obvious to both DaRon and Taleed that Candice had been beaten, choked and who knows what else.

"I didn't know he would show up here." Tears steadily fell from her eyes. Taleed's mouth fell open as he pulled her trembling body into him, attempting to console her. Her frail body shook uncontrollably. Gently, he stroked her back. She jumped as if startled by his touch. She was in pain and at that moment, both Taleed and DaRon were also.

"Who Candice?" Taleed spoke in a whisper. "Who showed up?"

"Nicolas," she sobbed his name. He stopped rubbing her back as the anger within intensified.

"That bitch-ass did this to you?" Taleed asked while pulling her away. She didn't answer as she had said too much as it was. Candice was afraid of what Taleed was going to do. "Candice, Nicolas did this to you?"

"We got into an argument about me visiting and not coming to see him. He wanted me to come back to his place." That was a lie but she couldn't tell him the real truth.

"That's it!" Taleed said after releasing her from his embrace. Then he turned around, but DaRon stood in front of him blocking his path. "Get the—

"I know what you thinking and I'm not lettin' you leave. Don't do it man."

"You see this shit!" Taleed yelled while pointing towards Candice. "And you want to stop me from going after his punk ass?"

"Taleed please don't do anything. All I want is for this to be over. DaRon, please talk to him." Candice pleaded.

Then DaRon said to him, "What I'm saying man is chill, cool out for a minute."

"That motherfucker is a dead man! Bet!"

"Candice, pack your bags." DaRon turned to her and continued. "Let's go. We're taking you home with us tonight."

"You know what man," Taleed said while walking towards the door. "You two go, I'm not letting this shit go without kicking his ass." He walked out.

"Taleed!" DaRon yelled and at the same time followed Taleed outside. "C'mon, let's think this through." Taleed ignored him and kept walking. "Oh, so you goin walk ten miles to his place?"

"I would be driving if your ass didn't hop in this big-ass gas guzzler." Taleed stopped walking and stared up at the dark sky. Sweat rolled down the side of his face.

"Try to calm down man."

"This is some bullshit!" Taleed pounded his fist on the hood of the vehicle and said between gritted teeth, "I wanna fuckin' kick that muthafuckin' ass."

"So do I, but I can't let you do something stupid like that."

"I already warned that bitch once before."

"And you made your point. I hate seeing her like this too."

"Why the fuck is she always protecting him? I won't ever understand that girl! She so-so – Urg!"

"Candice, man she gotta soft heart. She don't want to see anyone she knows be hurt, even if it is the person who beats on her."

"Yeah, just wait until I get to that ass. And I will get him, maybe not tonight but watch me, I'll get him."

"That's another reason for her not wanting to get you involved. Hell, I'd like to give him a beat down for doing her like that."

"Then let's do this. We know where his punk-ass live. It's not like –

"You sick dude. First you chase him down the block and pistol whoop his ass, then you steal his ride. Now you wanna roll up there in the fuckin' middle of the night like some ninja and get revenge for beating up your son's mother. No man, I ain't doin' it." The two of them watched as Candice slowly walked towards them dragging her overnight bag. She was trying to conceal the pain but did a horrible job of it. They could tell she was hurting.

Chapter 22

It was after three in the morning when DaRon pulled his SUV in front of the multi-family unit that he rented out to Candice. After he turned off the engine, Taleed hopped out of the passenger's side.

"Help me get her inside the apartment," he said to DaRon after lifting Candice from the elevated vehicle. She was sound asleep.

Once they walked inside of her apartment, he laid her tiny frame in the center of the queen size bed. It seemed to consume her. She never stirred. After removing her shoes, Taleed pulled the comforter over her before leaving the room. DaRon was waiting for him in the next room.

"What're you gonna do now?" he asked Taleed.

"I haven't figured that out yet, but I'm staying here tonight."

"Yeah, I think that's a good idea. I'll come by in a few hours with your car."

"I appreciate everything, man." They shook hands and embraced before DaRon exited the apartment. Taleed's body was beginning to feel the fatigue from the previous day's events. He returned to the bedroom and noticed that Candice never moved from the spot he initially laid her.

He had only intended to lie down and briefly rest his eyes but when he was awakened by his vibrating cell phone, it was eight o'clock in the morning. He was staring down at the top of Candice's head. She was nestled in the middle of his chest. Gently, he rolled her onto the center of the bed. Her eyes opened.

"What's going on? Where you going?"

"Go back to sleep," he said before leaving the room. When he answered the call, it was Kendra. He had forgotten that he told her he was going to be stopping by last night. In the past, he'd never had to explain his relationship with his son's mother to her. That may have to change. Taleed felt he needed to spend more time with Candice. He didn't want what happened to her to ever happen again, and he was going to make sure of it.

"As soon as I get some things situated, I'll be there. I'll call you when I'm on the way." He didn't tell Kendra where he spent the night. It wasn't necessary. Kendra may never understand that what he felt for Candice had nothing to do with the feelings he had her.

Candice came in the living room just as he ended the call. "Where's my son?"

"He's with Mac. You should get some rest. I'll bring him home later." He watched her walk away. "Candice, I really don't like the decisions you seem to making. This man beat the—"

She stopped, then turned to him, "Don't lecture me."

"It's not a lecture, it's a fact. That bitch tried to beat the shit outta you and probably would have killed you. Look at those bruises around your neck."

"I don't wanna talk about it, Taleed."

"Look at you. Lil' man count on you to be there for him and you go off running to North Carolina chasing after some—"

"Like I told you before," she raised her voice, "I went to see my family!"

186

"No! You went to North Carolina and let some punk put his hands on you."

"I didn't go to see him." Candice didn't want to tell him the real reason she went to North Carolina; it was personal and she didn't want to tell him about it.

"Well then, how did he know you were there?"

"Stay out of my business!"

"Huh? Stay outta what? You didn't say that yesterday when you got your ass beat. Did you say that last night when you were snuggling next to me like a little lost puppy dog."

She turned and walked inside the bathroom, slamming the door behind her.

"It could have been worse!" Taleed yelled after she closed the bathroom door. "Candice!" he yelled her name before pounding a fist on the door. "You goin' come out sooner or later. And guess what, Imma be right here. Candice!"

The door flung open and she said, "Why can't you just leave me alone, Taleed? I want this-this to all go away. Please, just go. Leave."

"I'm not leaving you alone because I care about you. I do Candice. I care about you a lot." Taleed leaned into her before reaching for her hand.

"Don't you need to be caring about Kendra, the one who keeps blowing up your phone?"

"She can take care of herself. I'm not sure you can."

She whispered, "I can, Taleed. You don't understand what I've been going through." Taleed knew Candice had some health issues but after she starting seeing a therapist she appeared to be getting much better.

"That's—

DaRon cleared his throat and asked, "Am I interrupting something?" He used his key to open the door and stood by it when he saw the two of them engaged in conversation. "Yo dude, I drove your car here."

Taleed lightly touched the side of Candice's cheek and said, "Get some rest." Then he kissed it. "I'll be back this afternoon with Lil' Man, aiight?" Then he and DaRon walked out of the unit.

188

Once they were inside the vehicle, DaRon asked him, "What's going on between you and Candice?"

"What?"

"There seems to be a whole lot of tension between you two and I'm not talking 'bout that heated kinda shit you had with her. This is like heated but, I dunno, more tension--sexual."

Taleed smacked his lips and said, "Oh, what now you some relationship therapist? She need help man. I was tryna reassure her, ya know, calm her down. I don't want her acting crazy when I bring Lil' Man back."

"Don't act like you... Dude, I know you getting some ass."

"Yeah, and it's not from her either. Not that it's any of your business, but I'm kinda seeing somebody, aiight?"

"I'm just saying?'

"What are you saying?" Taleed asked and then said, "I ain't think so."

DaRon decided not to ask any more questions and the two rode to his home in silence. In the back of his mind, Taleed knew that DaRon wasn't through with his interrogation. This was not the right time to go into detail about his relationship.

Chapter 23

As he entered Route 50, KC's cell phone vibrated. He glanced at the Bluetooth window on the dash of his vehicle and noticed it was Felicia.

"What's up, sexy?"

"Wanna get a drink?"

"Name the place and I'm there."

He was glad she didn't want to meet in the city because he'd had enough of it for one week. When KC walked inside JPs, he spotted her sitting at the bar looking as lively as she did the last time he left her.

"Starting without me I see," he said and then sat at the stool next to her. He nodded up as the bartender placed his drink in front of him.

"Good to see you, too." she said when KC placed a kiss on her cheek and reached for his drink. "Long day, huh?"

He huffed and said, "Yeah. I really need this break." Then added, "you looking hot, ma."

Three drinks later and after the small talk, Felicia practically invited herself back to his place.

"I have the whole weekend to myself. I don't have to go back to work until Sunday night." Felicia is a live-in health care provider to an elderly woman who resides in Malton.

"Hummm. How'd you get here? Did you drive or did you take the Metro?"

"I drove. But I can follow you home." KC smiled and motioned for the check.

"So this is who you been spending your time with? I thought you were too swamped with business to be in a serious relationship! You lying bastard!" Then she turned to Felicia and said, "You know he's going to screw you over after he gets what he want."

For a moment, KC ignored the interruption and handed his credit card to the bartender who noticed his urgency.

"Parker? Are you done?" KC said not wanting an answer.

"I just think it's fucked up how you did me. And you know it. I was good to you and didn't deserve to be treated like that by you. Un huh, is this the chick who you gave the ring to?"

"We already talked about that, and like I told you before, it's none of you business." He signed the receipt and shoved the credit card inside his pocket. "Lets go." KC stood to escort his date from the bar. Parker was causing a scene and he wanted nothing more but to get as far away from it as possible.

"Where's the ring?" Parker asked Felicia, blocking her path.

"Don't answer her," KC said quickly and at the same time reached for Felicia's arm. He pulled her to the opposite side, away from Parker while trying to make an exit.

In the back of her mind, Felicia wondered if he had actually given someone else a ring or was this girl a scorned lover. It didn't matter to her because she was going home with him. *Someone else may fall for that, but not this chick.* Felicia thought.

Parker followed and then added, "If you ain't wearing it, somebody else is. Somebody else is wearing a two thousand dollar Tiffany ring. Girl, don't say you didn't know."

Once KC and Felicia reached her car, he took her keys, unlocked and then opened the door. She slid inside the driver's seat. He leaned in to peck her lips ignoring the fact that Parker stood behind watching.

"I hope that didn't kill the mood."

"Absolutely not," she responded. *Ah, this one may be a keeper,* he thought. He smiled, happy to know that Parker's outburst didn't spoil his plans with Felicia.

"I'll make it up to you." Felicia knew that he would somehow do what he had to do to make her forget this moment. She had already filed it in the back of her mind. Nothing was going to come between what she wanted. KC was one man she wanted.

He closed her door after she started the engine and walked past Parker, ignoring her seething stares.

She mumbled, "Go to hell you son-of-a-bitch."

KC kept walking towards his vehicle but replied by sticking out his middle finger.

After walking inside his condo, KC felt Felicia's tight hug around his waist. She laid her head in the center of his back.

"You want something to drink?" he asked.

"Who was that girl?" she asked KC. He knew that question was lingering in the forefront.

He turned to face her. "We dated briefly. But she's much older, and after a few months, we kind of didn't click no more." He pecked her lips and said, "I don't want to talk about her. As a matter of fact, I don't want to talk at all." He pulled her into him and passionately kissed her. Felicia wrapped her arms around his neck when he lifted her, and walked toward his bedroom. He released her long enough to remove her blouse. She wiggled out of the skirt and then helped him undress. KC shielded himself then sat and grabbed both her upper thighs pulling her on top of him. She placed a knee on the bed, reached for his member and inserted it inside her moistness. KC moaned as he toyed with one nipple using his thumb and forefinger. The other, he sucked on it, lightly nibbled on it, and tongued danced with it. Felicia was enjoying bouncing up and down on his manhood and

195

was close to an orgasm, but KC stood and planted her firmly on the bed. He pulled her legs up and over his shoulders and was slamming his rod inside her. She wanted to cry out in pain but it felt good at the same time. Then he climbed on the bed, stretched out until her legs were above her head and dug his member inside deeper. She moaned her orgasm uncontrollably as KC grunted his.

He collapsed next to her, trying to catch his breath. Satisfied, she, too, was breathing heavily. Felicia turned to him and wiped the sweat from his face. She smiled when he opened his eyes.

KC puckered his lips to simulate a kiss and said, "Spend the night with me."

She didn't answer. Felicia cuddled next to him and sleep quickly took over.

The next morning a vibrating cell phone awakened KC. He reached over Felicia, assuming it was his and grabbed it from his pant pocket. It was Chance. "Yo, whadup?" he said in a raspy voice. He looked at his watch. It was seven in the morning and he did not like the urgency in his partner's voice.

Chance knew that he had to relieve KC of his duties of CEO at Keon-Chance Technologies and he had to do it sooner than later.

KC wiped the sleep from his eyes and looked at his sleeping mate. Gently, he planted kisses on her shoulder until she stirred. It was a welcomed gesture, and Felicia smiled.

"Wake up," he whispered. She moaned as he stroked her shoulders. "I got something for you." Then he pulled a wrapper from under the pillow, unrolled it on his manhood and eased it inside of her warmth. KC hurriedly pumped himself between the walls of her moistness until he skirted his load inside the plastic barrier.

When he had a moment to settle his breathing and the blood returned to the places where it had left, KC slid off the bed and said, "Now get up. I got somewhere to be in twenty minutes."

Felicia didn't like hearing those cold words coming from a man who just made love to her. She had plans of sleeping in and spending the day with him. She thought about asking him to let her stay until he returned but decided against it. He had

197

already left the room as she could hear running water coming from the bathroom.

Chapter 24

His brother's words played around in his mind repeatedly. Chance didn't like the idea of having to meet his friend this early in the morning to hand him his exit papers from the company.

KC didn't ask any questions when Chance had called him so early even though he'd preferred to be snuggled up to his overnight guest. It never occurred to him that Chance wanted to meet at the coffee house, even though he was a workaholic, so KC didn't ask any questions during the phone conversation. He assumed this meeting had nothing to do with business.

Chance was sitting with his back to the door when KC walked towards the table. Chance stood after noticing from his peripheral view that someone was walking in his space. Without speaking, the two of them reached for the other's hand and simultaneously were pulled into a brotherly embrace.

"Can I take your order?" The waitress had come over to the table after noticing another customer had taken a seat at one of her tables.

"Just coffee, thanks." KC noticed the stern look on Chance's face. "What's going on?" His cell phone buzzed. KC looked at the display to see that it was a text message from Felicia.

"When we started this process months ago, there was a certain level of commitment that we both knew and everyone at Tech knew we were up against. I had a meeting with Maxwell –

"Without me?" KC interrupted.

"Yeah without you because the meeting was about you. The problem is members on the board don't believe you take your role in this company serious."

"What?!"

"KC, you're CEO at this company that investors, members, certain groups are looking at riding us…" he paused when the waitress returned with a cup and poured coffee inside of it.

"They know about all the women you've been messing around with and that does not look good and taints your character."

"Oh, so now we goin look at the women in my life now?"

"Your character is being questioned because of all this running around. Hell, you got like three, four women in and out of your bed and got like one, maybe two, stalkers."

"Stalkers? Chance, really?"

"Yeah. She got you running out of the county because you can't control her. I see how you look at your phone when it rings. Remember you called me when she slashed your tires. That girl is causing you a whole lot of headache. KC, if Rocky knows about the shit that you doin' and he's concerned enough to pull me to the side, it's serious. Serious enough that he knows if it weren't for your philandering, Tech could sail through this offering without any problem. It was recommended that you remove yourself from the company at least until this public offering is over."

"You're asking me to step down? Is that what you're saying?"

"Hey, after everything is over, things can go back to where they were. You get your title back without losing any interests. Everything goes back to way it's always been. I don't want to have to do this the legal way because I know your concern is for Tech to succeed and we're close to the finish line."

Chance paused and stared as his friend slowly lifted his coffee cup. He took a sip and met Chance's stare before saying, "I own half of Tech."

"Yes, you do. And you still will when this is all settled."

He slammed the cup loudly on the table. Patrons and some of the wait staff nearby stared in their direction and the loud sound caused Chance to sit upright. "Bullshit! Why the fuck would you think I would just walk away? If I own half of Tech."

"I'm not asking you to walk away. It was suggested that you step down and disassociate yourself with the company until we go—"

"You want competition? You got it cause I can run my own company without you or anyone else you got at Tech."

"Let's not do this, alright? You getting all worked up for nothing. If you just go along with what Rocky suggested, Tech can go through this transition easily."

"Do you think I'm going to let you kick me out of the company? Man, I have a lot invested in this company and if you want me out, you're going to have to buy me out. I ain't going nowhere."

"KC, you don't understand man, we can't get any attorneys involved because it would halt our position with the public offering."

"Oh, so you think I'm just going to give up my status as CEO without—"

"Briefly, KC. Just until the company goes public." Chance said each word carefully. He was running out of patience with his argumentative friend. He remembered what his brother said and the advice he had given Chance. *Don't get angry and don't get him angry because the situation could get ugly. Don't let this get out of hand.*

"Fuck this shit." KC stood and while walking towards the door, mumbled, *I leave my warm bed and a piece of ass for this bullshit.*

He heard Chance say, "Get some help, KC. This is not normal for a grown-ass man." Then he walked out of the coffee shop without saying another word. Chance pulled out his wallet, laid two five-dollar bills on the table and followed KC. By the time he reached the door, Chance spotted KC's vehicle leaving the parking lot.

Chapter 25

Once he left the coffee house, he jogged down the steps towards the parking lot. KC pressed the button on the keyless remote to release the lock on the car door. Once he sat inside, he banged his fist on the dash.

"Damit! Fuck!" He was livid, and at the moment too irrational to understand why his business partner, his best friend would remove him from his position as CEO when he's held it for many years. KC ran that company for years when Chance left the States for Germany to do research in the technology field. He was the one who took over the business when Chance left the country after graduation for almost five years and then took off for two weeks on his honeymoon. Not once did he leave his business partner and best friend when he needed him most. And now, this is the "thanks" he gets. He drove from the coffee house not knowing where he was going, but he had to drive to get as far away as possible before he did something he would live to regret. After driving the capital beltway for over an hour, he pulled his vehicle in front of his residence, but instead of exiting, KC chose to sit and think. *I can do this. Yeah, I can start my own company.* "Shit! Fuck it!" he said aloud before exiting the vehicle. When he got inside, he tossed his keys on the table and immediately reached for the Crown Royal bottle and a glass. KC poured himself a drink and sat at the bar, staring into space wondering where he went wrong. *Well let me see, there's that Parker chick who wouldn't take "no" for an answer until I practically tossed her naked ass out of my house. Then that bitch Lucky tried to set me up to being robbed. Then there's Felicia who could have been in lead position if it were not for her sending me those five text messages this morning talking about how much she miss me and can't wait to be with me. Damn, it was only minutes after leaving her ass. Then I just had to have me a little chocolate drop like Deanna. Oh and I can't forget that stalking-ass nut case Alex who slashed my fuckin' tires, is following me around town and now won't leave me the fuck alone. Yeah, maybe the list of foolishness I carried on with these crazy women is getting a little long.* He poured another drink, pulled his cell phone from his pocket and scrolled through the list of Contacts until he found her name.

"What's up, sexy lady?"

Hearing his voice made her giddy, but every time he called, she was either with a client or on her way to meet one. *Dag! Bad timing again, KC.* She thought to herself. "KC. It's good to hear from you, but I'm kind of in a rush right now."

"Ah c'mon, ma. I know you gotta minute."

Jade never turned him down because not only was he generous, KC was one fine brother. What woman in her right mind would say "no" to someone like him? She had to admit, he was much better looking than most of regulars at the escort service. She thought about calling her client to cancel, but the madam would give her hell if that ever happened.

When he opened the door to his condominium, KC was shirtless, wearing only a pair of faded jeans, and because he didn't have a belt, they were sagging dangerously low. He stared at her and said, "Damn, you look so good."

Jade was wearing a thin, white, low-cut blouse with a black mini skirt and red stilettos. KC admired her shapely frame as he stood to the side and motioned for her to enter, still holding the Crown Royal bottle.

Jade walked inside his home, not once taking her eyes off him.

"I could say the same about you. You're not looking too bad yourself." She scanned his frame from the top of his shaven head to his bare chest, washboard abs, and down to the bulge protruding from his jeans.

Before she could put down her bag, KC pulled her into him and stroked her backside. She wasn't wearing anything under her mini skirt. She pulled it upward so that he could get a better feel of her nakedness. Jade reached for the button of his trousers, stuck her hand inside to feel the massive bulge urging for an escape. She pushed him towards the sofa while sliding his jeans down. Once he landed on the sofa, Jade slid the jeans down his legs and positioned herself between them. She gently inserted his firm member inside her mouth and sucked on it. KC inhaled sharply when she licked the tip and made circular motions with her tongue. Then Jade re-inserted his dick inside her mouth, and then using a firm grip, began stroking it up and down. With each stroke, Jade could feel the veins on his member pulsate and expand. This, to her was a turn-on. She could sense his ejaculation building but was surprised when KC suddenly pushed her away and positioned himself behind her while still on her knees.

"Hey!" she began to protest knowing what he was about to do. KC liked being the dominant partner during sex. "I don't have time—"

But, before she could finish what she wanted to say, KC grabbed a hand full of her hair, shoved her head between the cushions of the sofa, shielded himself and inserted his dick inside of her from the rear.

"Shhhh. This won't take long." KC started pumping himself inside of her until he released his orgasm. After only a few seconds of heavy breathing from both of them, he pulled out of her, released the grip he had on her hair, and stood. The two began to redress in the middle of the room. Jade attempted to make herself as presentable as possible given the fact that her hair had lost the majority of its curls and her makeup was now smeared. After handing her some folded bills, KC followed her to the door; No further words were exchanged. When the door closed shut, KC leaned his head on it and said, "And to add to that list of foolishness, I can't believe I just paid a hooker for a piece of ass. Fuck!"

He walked towards the couch and slumped down. He'd never felt this low in his life. Then he thought, *I've gotta work on me. I need to get my life in order.*

Chapter 26

Two days after being handed his walking papers, KC calmed down a bit but was still heated with his former business partner. He wanted to pick up the phone and tell his friend where to take that company and what he really felt about being his partner. But it would all be a lie. He loved working alongside Chance and had become extremely close to Tricia who had become a valuable commodity to the company. KC poured everything he had in the company, and now after so many years of brainstorming, creating, designing and delivering some of the high-tech gadgets together, it has all come to an end for him.

It was early Saturday afternoon, and for the first time in months KC had no place to go and nothing to do. Everything up to this point was running smoothly. Tech was on its way to being traded publically and it was up to the attorneys to make sure that all ends met.

All of this would happen while KC was basically on a two-month suspension with pay.

He decided to pay DaRon a visit. KC wanted an independent party to talk to about what he had been delivered; a pink slip from the company he worked so hard at making it the success it had become.

"Yo, what's up, potna?" DaRon greeted him when he opened the door. The two shook hands and embraced then KC walked in.

"Man, I got some issues."

"We goin hit the court tomorrow or what. Man y'all mugs are tripp'n." The fellows hadn't played their weekly pickup game in months because of the busy schedules.

"For real, man, your boy is tripp'n. I don't think that's going to happen anytime soon. Whoa, what's this?" KC pointed to the little person sitting on the sofa pulling on a fruit snack.

"Yeah, he's like a staple around here. Mac's got me watching him until she comes back. I don't mind, it forces me to catch up on some paperwork."

"What up, Lil' man?" KC said to Taleed's son and then offered him a fist. He decided to forgo

212

mentioning his dilemma with DaRon for a later time.

The child tapped it and said, "Hi, Uncle KC."

"So how long you gotta watch him? I was thinking about hitting JPs for a drink."

"She otta be back real soon. But I really need to check on some of the properties when she does—well speak of the devil."

KC looked over his shoulder and was pleasantly surprised to see Shaeterra walk inside the condo following MacKenzie. They both were carrying large Macy's bags.

"Hey, baby." MacKenzie said to DaRon and pecked his cheek. Then turned to KC, "Hey you. Good to see you again." KC winked at her.

"Hey, baby girl." KC said to Shaeterra.

She smiled, then asked, "What're you doing here?" She hugged KC.

"Came by for a visit, that's all."

"Hey you guys should stay for dinner. We're having Chicken Nuggets," MacKenzie said while looking at Taleed's son. He grinned.

"Oh yummy." KC was being flippant. "That sounds like fun but why don't we hit up D&B?" he said to Shaeterra. "If you're interested, I'd love to beat you in a few games."

"Beat me? I don't think so, mister. But yeah, I'd like that."

"Oh sure. Go when you know we can't go," MacKenzie kidded.

"Next time, sweets," KC said to MacKenzie and then asked Shaeterra, "You ready?"

"Yep. I'll call you tomorrow, Mac," Shaeterra said and then handed her the Macy's bags.

"Later, Lil' man," KC said. Then told DaRon, "See you at the gym tomorrow, dude." He took Shaeterra by the arm and led her out of the home.

When they got to KC's vehicle, he opened the passenger door and watched her sit, and once he got inside, she looked at him with smiling eyes.

"What?" KC grinned.

"You knew I would be over to Mac's house, didn't you?"

He laughed. "No. No I didn't."

"Yeah right." She didn't believe him.

After showing their IDs to the attendants

monitoring the door at D&B, both KC and Shaeterra walked towards the ticket counter. "Somebody's getting a butt whopping tonight," KC said when he handed the attendant two twenty dollar bills. She smiled at him.

"Oh yeah? How much you wanna bet?" Shaeterra challenged.

"I don't wanna bet you girl. I'm 'bout to show you who I am." He handed her half the tickets. "Where you want to start? Ops. Why don't we try the hoops?" The last time they were at D&B Shaeterra couldn't make one basket until KC gave her shooting techniques.

"Oh, I see what you're trying to do. You think you can beat me playing ball because I didn't do so good the last time."

"Naw, I'm just saying. Then you pick what game you wanna play."

"It's cool. Basketball it is. C'mon, I'm not afraid of a challenge." KC waited for her to pick up a ball before reaching for one of his own.

"Ladies first." She aimed for the rim and released. The shot made it through. "Ah snap. Check you out, Ms. Thang."

"What? Don't mess with me," she bragged as KC took his turn. His shot went through the net.

"Let's see what you got now, shorty." She made her second and third shot. When they totaled the score Shaeterra had five baskets made to KC's eight baskets. "What's next?" he asked her.

"Daytona USA! Yes!"

"I'll watch you."

"Scared? Huh, KC? You scared I'm going to beat you?"

"Absolutely not. I'm six four. I don't fit in that little cage. But go ahead, I'll watch you crash against the wall." She smacked his arm before climbing inside the shell. He stood outside of it and watched her steer her simulated racecar around the curvy, bumpy raceway and after she crashed, KC took it as an opportunity to make fun of her lack of driving skills.

"Damn Shae, you tore up that wall. In real life they'd be using tweezers to pick up your remains off the pavement. Move over, let me show you how it's done." KC slid inside the simulated game inching her away from the seat. She laughed at him because he had to hunch over just to fit in the small encasement. It was tricky for him driving the animated racecar wasn't much better than her driving, so when the game was over, KC crawled out. This time it was Shaeterra's turn to tease him.

"Un-huh. See, you thought it was easy didn't you? What was your score?" She attempted to peep inside but KC grabbed her around the waist.

"Get outta there. Can't you see that kid waiting to play?"

"You're so wrong, KC."

"Yeah, I know. I'm hungry, you?"

Looking around the game room, KC managed to get the attention of a passing waitress who ushered them to an empty table. When they finished with dinner, they played Artic Thunder and hydro-Thunder before leaving the game room.

Before the two got to the mall exit, there was a kiosk with fresh floral arrangements on display. KC stopped and purchased a vase containing six long stem roses. He sniffed them.

"These are for my mother," he said to Shaeterra

217

after paying the cashier.

"That's so sweet," she said and then he handed her the vase.

"Is this my punishment for losing in Nothing But Net? I have to carry your purchases?"

"No. I lied. These are for you, sweetheart." After thanking him, she reached up and hugged him tightly. KC wasn't expecting the kiss she planted on his lips, but nonetheless, it was a pleasant surprise.

When KC pulled inside the apartment complex, Shaeterra said, "Come in. I want you to see my new place." She moved from the apartment shared with the two roommates especially because of the lack of respect from them. They would constantly prance around in their underwear whenever KC came to visit. It was a nice show, but KC was not the least interested in either one of them.

Once she opened the door and flipped on the lights, KC was impressed with her décor. "Nice," he said while looking around the small space.

"You like?" Shaeterra smiled as he walked towards the kitchen separated by a granite barrier. A small wine rack sat at the end of the bar. KC took out a bottle of wine that was familiar to his taste.

"Did you plan this?" he asked.

"What?"

"Are you trying to seduce me? I mean 'cause you know this is my favorite right here."

Shaeterra reached for two wine glasses and sat them on the counter. After moving into her one bedroom apartment, she picked up several bottles of wine knowing that it was KC's favorite. She was hoping he'd notice the bottle.

Soon, he was pouring the last drop of wine into the glasses.

"Wow. Did we just kill that bottle?" He looked at Shaeterra and gently rubbed her cheek. "Thanks for spending the day with me."

She smiled and rested her head on his shoulders, closed her eyes and said, "Um, that was so good."

"It could be better." KC rubbed her shoulders and kissed the top of head trying to get her to give in to his advances. What surprised KC is when she looked up at him and pecked his lips. "You know it's okay if you want to seduce me, take advantage of me after all of this wine we just had. I wouldn't hold it against you."

"Drive safely, KC." She said, knowing that he was being facetious. The three words he didn't want to hear this night, but he didn't want to force her into doing something she wasn't ready to do. But when will she be ready? *At least let a brotha get a sniff, a lil' sample, or something.* KC's patience was getting thinner by the minute. But then he remembered something his former partner said to him. *Get some help, KC. This is not normal for a grown-ass man.* Maybe Chance was right; him wanting sex with so many women was maybe extreme, and for this same reason, Shaeterra was off-limits. She thought too much of herself to become involved with a man who wouldn't or didn't know how to settle down with one woman.

It was well after eight when he left Shaeterra's apartment, and as soon as KC walked inside his condo, his cell phone vibrated. He retrieved it from his pocket and looked at the display. It was a text message that read:

`Thx KC. Can't wait to c u again.`
`Shae`

What? The heck? KC asked himself. The message was confusing but before he could analyze its meaning, the phone rang.

"This is Keon." He said not recognizing the number shown on the display.

"So is that your latest conquest?" It was Alex.

Damn! KC cursed. "Stop fucking following me, dammit! Is you crazy?" He wanted to take back that question as soon as the words left his mouth. He already knew the answer.

"You keep ignoring my messages."

"Ah duh. Why in the hell are you still calling me?"

"Because I want to talk to you. I want to see you, KC." She began sobbing her words hoping it would warm his heart. It didn't.

"Hell fucking no! Like I told you before, there ain't shit to talk about, there ain't shit between us and there never will be. Now stop harassing me!" he said loudly into the receiver and then pressed the End key.

She had only been in the state of Maryland for two months. With only a high school education and the clothes on her back, Alex left home, the Parish of

Pleasant Hill, Louisiana, population just under eight hundred, in search of her dream. Like all the other girls back home, she wanted to marry money and KC was the man she wanted to fulfill her dreams. One way or another, she was going to do what was needed to be done to secure her future with him. There was no way she was returning to that small parish. She set out for the city and so far with so many opportunities it had to offer her decision was the right decision.

Chapter 27

After collecting rent on two of his rental units, DaRon steered his vehicle in the direction of his best friend's home. They hadn't had the weekly game of basketball in weeks, mostly because of two missing players, Chaz and Hakim, but the friction between KC and Chance made it even harder to even pick up a straggler. Just as always, he pulled in front of the opened double car garage, turned off the engine and stepped out. Joelee greeted him at the side door.

"Hey you? What brings you out here?" DaRon would only visit Chance if something was serious enough that it could only be said face to face. Joelee knew this to be true.

"Jo. Whaddup, baby girl? Heard you was over the house the other day," he said to Joelee. Then turned to Chance. "What's up dawg?" Chance was sitting at the bar pounding away on his laptop. He held out his fist to DaRon.

"Have a seat." He said without taking his eye off the screen. Somehow Chance knew DaRon wanted to inquire about their lack of interaction since Tech took on a different path.

"I tried to wait for you, but Mac said you weren't going to be back for a few hours."

"That's cool." DaRon responded but quickly turned his attention to Chance when Joelee walked away. "You gotta minute to chat?"

Chance didn't answer. He just stared at DaRon. Sooner or later, he knew his friend would also drill him about severing his business relationship with KC. Both KC and DaRon were as close as friends as the two of them. But there was no way Chance was going to discuss his business with DaRon. He never had in the past. Surely he didn't expect him to. He slid his stool away from the bar and stood.

"Let's talk outside."

Joelee who had her back to the two friends turned around to face them after hearing that her husband wanted to have a private conversation. What he did reminded her of the conversation she had with MacKenzie. *I'm his wife and he should trust me and not have any secrets. Like you and Chance, you guys share everything because he trusts you.* Apparently, not quite everything.

"Chance, you can talk around me. I *am* your wife."

He walked out of the room without responding. Joelee stared at his back and watched DaRon follow behind. This infuriated her and she made a mental note to speak to him about his attitude, which lately had been sour.

When they got outside, Chance leaned against DaRon's vehicle, and before he could speak, DaRon asked, "What's that all about? You just ignore her like that?"

"You can thank your wife. Somehow she and Joelee think we're holding shit from them."

"Oh, so that answers my question why Mac said me and her ain't having anymore secrets."

Then Chance said, "I know why you're here, man, and whatever went down with Tech was done out of necessity. I know KC made it seem worse than it really is but it had to be done."

"What about your friendship, man. He's talking about you being a non-factor and how he can take—"

"It's all talk, alright? You know how KC can be. He's like a whiny little bitch sometimes." Chance was getting frustrated by the minute. "Look I don't want to hear about it nor do I want to talk about it, okay? I got enough stress with this public offering. You need anything else?" Chance stood upright and started to walk away. "Go home to your wife. I hear you haven't been spending a whole lot of time there."

"Yeah, but I'm there when I'm there. She's making it hard, but the good thing is we both like having Taleed's son around."

"Maybe you should start on your own family."

DaRon gave him a quizzical look, then Chance added, "Look, you fucked up dude. You're still holding on to a dead girl, and your wife knows it. If she could dig that bitch up and whoop her ass she'd do it, but for now, all she's got is you to beat up—"

"She was my friend!" DaRon yelled at him, referring to Nevada Majuave, his now deceased college friend.

"Bullshit! You was fucking that girl!" Chance yelled back.

"Umph." DaRon grunted, still unable to digest reality to his past relationship with Nevada.

"And-and not only were you fucking her, you paid her tuition her last semester at the university. Yeah, I know about that," Chance added.

"That damn KC got a big fucking mouth."

"Nawww. It wasn't KC. Remember, Neva and my wife were good friends. She bragged about your generosity to my wife, you idiot, not KC."

Then DaRon said calmly, "Maybe I was. But I never touched her like that when me and Mac got together. Never."

"All I'm saying is, stay your ass home and make her feel like she's all that matters."

"Now you're giving marital advice?"

"You think I can't?"

"Your wife doesn't trust you, you don't trust her enough to share your life with her. Your business with her. You look like you mad at the world. Take your own advice and make Jo feel like she's all that matters. Don't you think she deserves that much?"

"Stay out of my business at my home and with my company."

"Jo was my girl before you even—"

"She's my wife—"

"All I know is from where I stand, your shit is looking pretty fucked up."

Chance knew there was some truth to what DaRon had said. Ever since the Offering, he had been on edge and to add insult to injury, having to terminate his best friend from Tech did not set well. His mood had been sour from the moment he had that discussion with Maxwell. That day had to have been the worst day of his life.

When he walked back inside his house from the garage, Joelee was chopping vegetables at the cutting board that was positioned over one side of the double sink. She didn't acknowledge him. He walked behind her and planted a kiss on the side of her neck.

"I love you, sweetheart, and I'm sorry but that was just something I needed to deal with."

"What was all the yelling about? I've never heard DaRon raise his voice like that before. What happened out there?"

"Nothing." Chance dismissed the questions from his wife

"Honey, I'm your wife and you should be able to talk around me without reservation. Me and DaRon have been friends for a very long time, you know this. I consider him a part of our family. How come you can't let me in your conversations you two have?"

"I'm sorry. I've been stressed with this public offering and things have happened that I didn't tell you about because I didn't feel comfortable discussing it with you or anyone at the time. That was the reason DaRon stopped by."

Lately, Chance's attitude had changed from the loving, caring husband he once was to more of a discombobulated shell of a man. He barely noticed her at times. She had been meaning to speak to him about this change, but it never seemed to be the right time.

She turned to face her husband and could not overlook the noticeable stress lines that had formed on his forehead. She could clearly see that something was bothering him and Joelee wanted to get to the cause of his stress.

"What is it, baby? she asked. "What happened?"

"I had to let KC go from Tech. The attorneys suggested we release him from his CEO duties because of some stuff he's been doing in his personal life. It's supposed to be only until Tech is public, but KC can be so fucking stubborn sometimes." He walked away rubbing his head.

"What do you mean stuff in his personal life? What does that have to do with Tech?"

"Everyone at Tech is being looked at under a microscope until this deal is done. We were all told that. KC ignored the warning. Without going into detail about his personal life, KC has just been doing some pretty shady shit, and it's come back to bite him in the ass. I swear that boy don't listen."

"Did you talk to him?"

"Yeah, when I gave him his termination papers a few days ago. Other than that, I can't talk to him anymore, not until this deal is done. To the investors, I represent Tech and for that I have to disassociate myself from him."

"He's your friend, baby."

Chance flopped on the sofa in the adjoining room. She followed and sat on his lap, wrapping both arms around him.

Chapter 28

The day after spending a fun-filled evening with Shaeterra, KC was lying on his bed staring up at the ceiling reflecting on their time together. *This girl is too young for me, but she is a lot of fun to be with. She sho' ain't givin' up no ass, that's for sho. What did that text mean? I can't wait to see you again. And what's with all the kissing? At the mall and later at her place. If she didn't want me to hit it, why not a friendly kiss on the cheek? No, she was kissing me on the lips.* "Hold up," he said out loud then sat upright.

At that moment, KC decided he needed clarification on these mixed signals he had been receiving from Shaeterra. She didn't think that what she was doing was misleading, she was too naïve to know that she was leading KC in believing that they were going to be intimate; maybe not in the immediate future, but eventually. He, on the other hand, didn't realize that his makeup gift, that ring he gave her in exchange for the graduation ring his mother had given him that he let her wear, meant more to her than it did to him. KC wasted no time in asking point-blank questions. As soon as the door to her apartment opened, he skipped the pleasantries and walked inside, closing the door behind him.

"I don't read minds." He reached for her but she stepped away from his grasp. "I came over to talk, Shae. Tell me what do you want from me?"

Shaeterra didn't expect for him to barge in with questions. This straightforwardness was all new to her. Quickly, she thought for a moment before saying, "I don't want you to be with that girl, um, um, Parker." Shaeterra knew her name but this was her way of stalling him. Clearly, he had caught her off guard.

"And then what, because I'm no longer with Parker."

"Well, those other girls that you've been seeing hanging out at JPs with. Every time I turn around one of my friends is telling me about some chick you were with."

"That's your problem, you listen to what other people say."

"Then you tell me it's not true." Shaeterra waited for him to answer.

But all KC said was, "We're not going to discuss other women when we're together."

"You haven't ended your relationship with that other woman, but you want me to share myself with you. That is so nasty. You think I'm going to be with a man knowing he's doing the same thing to another female?"

"I like you Shae, but I want to know what is it you want from me? That's why I'm here. You text me minutes after I left here. Why? Why couldn't you tell me what the text said to my face? How come you couldn't say 'I had a good time, KC or-or 'Can't wait to see you again, KC' while I was here, huh?"

"Well it's obvious I like you KC, but I want you to want me, and not those other women. But only if you're with me exclusively. Now you tell me, am I crazy? No, I'm not. I'm one woman who wants an exclusive relationship. Now what do you want?"

KC reached for her gently bringing her body into his. He toyed with strands of hair admiring her, this time close up. He leaned into her capturing her moist lips then slid his tongue across her bottom lip. She moaned when he parted her lips and playfully licked at her tongue. Then he recaptured her mouth, eagerly sucking her tongue into his own. Shaeterra didn't resist his advances. She was receptive, and KC could feel her trembling body. It was only then when he slowly pulled away, but not before planting faint kisses on her nose, forehead, and then back to her soft lips. She rested her cheek on his hand. Then he whispered, "What do I want? Shae, I want to feel your nude body next to mine. I want to show you the most passionate pleasure two people can share. Let me show you what I'm feeling, the emotions that's been building up in me, exclusively for you. What I want Shae, what I want is to make love to you."

"I want to know that you're through with those girls. All of them, not just that Parker girl."

"Right now Shae, I don't have the same feelings for any of them that I have for you. And that's the honest to goodness truth."

She lifted her head and looked at him. "I can't trust that. I'm not sure you're ready for an exclusive relationship with me. I can see you hurting me only because you want to sleep with me. I'm not trying to be hurt." KC walked away exhaling sharply. He sat on the sofa. Not only was he exhausted from everything he had gone through this week, losing his position as CEO of his company, being stalked by Alex and harassed by Parker at the bar, but being denied again by a woman who he couldn't seem to get off his mind.

She walked to where KC sat and instinctively he reached for her backside, pulling her hips into his face. She rubbed his head in return. KC closed his eyes and inhaled, hoping to receive much-needed relief from the internal ache he was feeling simply by smelling her. He nudged the bottom of the blouse with his mouth until her stomach was exposed. Then KC began lightly kissing her navel. He lowered the waist of her skirt until her bikini line was exposed.

"KC—" He kissed the uncovered area and slowly slid his fingers alongside the waist of her skirt, making contact with her flesh. She shuddered.

"Do you trust me?" he asked her. She stared down at KC. Her eyes were glossy. She did trust him, but she wasn't going to so easily give up her virginity to him if he was not going to commit to her. "I won't take what you won't give me." He waited for her to respond but all she did was stare down at him. KC started sliding her skirt down below her hips. He traced the front seams of her panties all the while stroking her moistness with roaming index fingers. She moaned. KC traced the seams to her backside once again, pulling her middle into him.

She reached for his hands that were busy massaging her rear passage while his tongue lightly massaged her front moistness through the thin material barricading restricted access.

"Tell me to stop, Shae, and I will." She said nothing, only began breathing heavily as he slid the annoying fabric down her slim hips. He stood and lifted her body, gently lowering her frame to the very spot where he previously sat. She released a soft sound of pleasure once he planted feather-like kisses on her virgin flesh. She trembled. The walls of her insides pulsated against his tongue that only rested at the entrance of her prize opening. The feeling was breathtaking, too good to stop, so KC started lapping at her outer folds, lightly sucking in her sweet juices as her body continued uncontrollably jerking and her pussy lips were beating against his tongue.

When her body relaxed, KC retreated, planting wet kisses on her stomach where he rested his head. For now this would have to do. He knew Shaeterra was not going to go any further, sexually that is.

"I would never ever hurt you, I can promise you that, Shae. You're an exceptionally beautiful woman that I respect too much to see you hurt. And I mean that," KC whispered into the warmth of her flesh.

Shaeterra was speechless. At this moment, she had no words. She felt relaxed, so relaxed that her body felt as light as a feather. This was the best feeling she had ever experienced in her entire life. Shaeterra had always heard that sex is like fireworks and that the feeling would be one she would remember for a lifetime. And even though what KC had just done to her was not the actual act of intercourse, it was in some form a sexual act that left her feeling content and totally at ease. There was something magical in what he just did to her that made Shaeterra want to be his girl forever. Certainly, she didn't want him to leave. She wanted to curl up in his arms and sleep throughout the night.

Chapter 29

K.C. was happy to pleasure her. It was all she was willing to relinquish. For what seemed like hours, his head rested on her stomach, deep in thought. When he looked up at her, Shaeterra was sound asleep. He stood and carried her inside her bedroom and laid her in the middle of the bed. She didn't move. KC sat on the edge of the bed. This was the first time he had been inside her bedroom. He looked around. The décor was as innocent as its decorator was. On one wall was a bookshelf filled with small stuffed animals, her college degree and a certificate from HU, but what caught his attention was the photograph sitting on the dresser. It was an old picture of him and Chance taken in 2006. He tilted his head. *I remember that picture. That was the year Chance came back from Germany. That night, me, DaRon, Taleed, Jo, and Candice were downtown at the Hard Rock Café celebrating Jo and Candice's graduation. I had to leave early 'cause I had to pick his ass up from Dulles. Instead of driving home, we met up with DaRon at Stan's for a drink to celebrate Chance's return. DaRon wasn't too happy because he had to drive the ladies back to their dorm and then come back to the city to meet with us. That knucklehead was showing off his new cell phone and had taken the picture with it.* KC smiled, remembering the moment and then asked himself, *How in the hell did she get that? Let me guess; Mac must have given it to her.*

"Aren't you going to stay with me?" Shaeterra startled him.

He thought long and hard about her question before answering, "No. I can't."

"Why?" She was confused.

"Why? Because if I stayed I'ma want more from you then what I just had and I know you not ready to give me anything else. Soooo, I have to leave. Although I don't want to, I have to."

"Are you going home so that you can be with somebody who will give you what you want?"

"Shae, out of respect for you and because I have to make some changes in my life, I'm going home to work on me. There're some things I need to make right in my life. I'll give you a call in the morning, alright? Maybe we can have brunch or something, take in a movie, I dunno, something. Is that alright with you?"

She smiled, "Yeah."

KC kissed her lips and stood. "Go back to sleep. I'll make sure to lock up on my way out." He left her apartment and jogged down the steps to where his vehicle was parked.

She watched as he pulled his vehicle in the parking space, careful not to be seen by anyone. Her body was hidden by the adjacent building. *That scum bastard, I know he was with her*, she thought. Alex waited until KC was inside the building before walking closer to the security door. She was going to stay close by until someone came in or out. After 20 minutes, the apartment building seemed quiet. She peeped inside and searched the long hallway. There was no movement from inside.

*You gotta be shit'n me. She actually watching his ass. Lemme...*Taleed picked up his cell phone and dialed KC's number. "Yo, dude. That bitch outside your building, peeping around the corner watching your ass."

"I told you she was crazy, man." KC answered.

"Aiight. I got something for that ass." Then he ended the call.

Not knowing what else she could do to get his attention, Alex pulled her cell phone from her oversized bag and dialed his number. The call went directly to voicemail. "Damit!" she cursed and then texted him a message hoping he would respond. After a few minutes her BBM indicated he had at least seen the message. This infuriated her even further. "Pick up the goddamn phone!" Alex yelled and then walked around the corner to where her vehicle was parked. Her mouth dropped at the sight ahead of her.

He backed up the sedan so that its rear was in the front of the small vehicle and popped the trunk. He didn't bother killing the engine, knowing his task wouldn't take very long. After exiting the vehicle, he reached inside the trunk to retrieve the lug wrench, hydraulic jack and a screwdriver. Taleed walked towards the driver's side of the small vehicle, dropped the hydraulic jack and lug wrench before stopping down to the front wheel. He pried the hubcap off and threw it inside of the sedan's trunk. Then walked towards the back and did the same. He repeated his actions on the passenger's side of the small vehicle. He pumped the hydraulic jack until the driver's side of the vehicle was fully raised. After removing the lug nuts he removed the tire and tossed it inside the trunk of the sedan. He repeated this for the remaining tires leaving the small vehicle resting on the frame. Three minutes later, he closed the sedan's trunk, shifted the gear to drive, drove down the block and waited. After a few minutes he spotted the head lights of the SUV in his rearview mirror coming towards him. *I knew you had it in you, dude.* Taleed thought of his friend.

What the heck happened to my car? Alex asked herself while walking around the vehicle. All four tires were gone and the frame was sitting on the pavement. Alex covered her mouth with both hands. She didn't know what to do or whom to call. She didn't have family here and if it weren't for the other waitresses at the bar she worked, Alex didn't have any friends. She looked to the right and then left. The street was deserted, except for one vehicle that was coming towards her. She hoped it would stop and when it did, she sighed in relief.

The driver rolled down his window and asked, "Is everything okay? Do you need some help?"

"Someone vandalized my car," Alex said almost in tears.

"Do you have roadside assistance? I mean, I can give you a ride to wherever you need to go."

She looked him over. His neatly tamed braids were protruding from his du-rag and besides he was nice enough to stop. To her he didn't look dangerous at all. "Can you give me a ride to my house? It's about 10 miles away. I can give you gas money."

"Get in. Looks like you've had enough bad luck tonight."

He drove the SUV out of the neighborhood towards a long stretch of highway that was dark and had no traffic lights. The nearest house on Powder Mill Road was eight miles ahead; the nearest gas station, four miles in the opposite direction. Once he got to what appeared the darkest part of the stretch of road, he pulled the vehicle to the side onto the gravel. Alex looked around, unsure of why he would suddenly stop in this particular area.

"What's wrong? Why'd you stop?"

Instead of answering, he retrieved a .9mm from beneath the driver's seat and pressed the barrel of it firmly against her temple. "Give me your purse."

Fear took over, "Here, take it. Please don't hurt me." She willingly handed her purse to him. If that's all he wanted, he could have it. "Just don't hurt me, please."

He fumbled around the clutter inside her purse until he located her wallet. In it, he took out her driver's license and tossed the purse and wallet back at her. Quickly she took them and nestled the items into her chest as if she was protecting a child.

"You hear this?" As he cocked the .9mm, it clicked, causing her to jump backwards towards the passenger door. "That's yours. If I see your ass anywhere near KC again, this bullet is going to be lodged in the back of that pretty little head of yours. This is your only warning, shorty. Stop stalking him and his peeps like you a fucking lunatic, ya hear? I know where you live." He held up the license. "And I will come for you. Now get your fucking ass outta my truck before I change my mind." Before Alex could fully exit the SUV, the driver gunned the engine and the tires roared as it sped through the darkness. As quickly as it sped off, the vehicle came to an unexpected stop. Alex watched in horror as the reverse lights illuminated. Her heartbeat quickened, as she was sure her life was about to end. Thinking the driver may have changed his mind, instinct took over and she began screaming hysterically. Alex turned, dropped her bag and wallet and bolted in the opposite direction. Not that anyone would hear her, there was nothing but blackness surrounding her. Not a single vehicle travelled this road during this time of night. Then she felt the rear of the two-ton vehicle make contact with her upper back and at the same time heard the screeching sound of tires against pavement. She was hit from behind, which forced her body to slam face-first on the pavement. She lay there motionless, moaning as the pain she was feeling was unbearable. Alex had a mouth full of blood and broken teeth. She spat not wanting to move because any movement would increase the pain she was feeling from her head to her lower back. When she managed to crawl out of the middle of the road, Alex could barely make out the faint taillights from the SUV as it sped through the night. That's when she passed out on the off-road gravel.

The driver of the SUV slowed its pace before crossing the red light cameras on the side of the road and picked up his cell phone. He punched in the two-digit code and spoke into the speakerphone. "I think that bitch tried to get a look at my tags. I had to take her out, but trust, it's done."

"My man," is all Taleed said before ending the call. Then he texted KC: Done!

Chapter 30

After hearing on the police scanner that the body found floating down the Potomac River was identified as Nicolas Glascoe, Candice's friend from North Carolina, Taleed headed to College Park earlier than he had planned. He wanted to know if Candice knew that Nicolas was even in town. His body lay in the morgue waiting for identification from his next to kin.

When she opened the door she was wearing an oversized sweatshirt that was used to wrap around Taleed's son late one night. It was left because Taleed didn't want to wake his son by slipping it over his head.

"So that's what happened to my Morgan State sweatshirt," Taleed said while walking inside the apartment. She closed the door and walked into the kitchen.

"I got cold. You want it back?" she asked before sitting at the bar.

"Naw, it's yours now." Her eyes shot dagger-like stares at him. "What? It's not like I can't get another one." It was a common item of clothing and Taleed knew if he wanted another MSU sweatshirt, he could stop by the school to pick up one. He lived only minutes from the campus.

"What do you want? Lil Taleed is sleeping." She appeared irritated.

"Did you know your boyfriend was in town?"

"He's not my boyfriend."

"Who else does Nicolas know in DC besides you?"

"Why do you always ask me about my friend?" She avoided eye contact and appeared nervous. Taleed noticed her nervousness but he continued pressuring her.

"Because I want to know who's around my son that's why?"

"Do you see me drilling you about your friend, Kendra?" She crossed her arms across her chest and stared at him waiting for an answer. Without emotion,

252

Taleed stared back. "Yeah, Lil Taleed talks about her a lot. He calls her Kenna. I figured because of that the two of you must be getting close."

"Your point?"

"I'm right, aren't I?" She smacked her lips. "I don't care to like, like drill you all the time about your friends because I don't really care who you seeing. I can tell he likes her and she obviously likes him. Damn Taleed, can't you give me the same credit?"

"I can. If you didn't run off to be with some dude that beat the shit outta you." She appeared uneasy but still he added, "Date somebody worthy to be around my son and I won't have to drill you."

"It's not that easy. I mean, good men are hard to find. Especially here in DC."

"Good men? Get real! Ain't nothing good about that motherfucka."

"You don't know him."

"Whatever. So when did you last see him?" She looked confused. "Nicholas? He's here you know."

"I didn't know."

"Have you seen him, Candice?"

253

"No, I haven't. Not since the last time when I went to see my parents."

"So, you mean to tell me your boyfriend is in town and you didn't know. You lying young." She stood and walked out of the kitchen. Taleed followed her to the bedroom and watched her nervously toss around some folded items on the bed.

"I'm tired, do you mind?"

"Yo? What you gotta hide?"

"I didn't know, alright?! Am I supposed to know every time he make a move? So what if he's in town? So what, Taleed?"

"So? Don't lie to me Candice. That's all I ask. Be honest wit me. Dag!"

Then as calmly as she could, Candice said, "Leave, Taleed."

"Since when do you tell me to leave?"

"Since this is my place!" She had had enough.

"Where I pay all the bills. You see Candice, you don't get to tell me to—"

"Get out!" she screamed at the top of her lungs. Taleed saw his son standing by the door. Their loud voices obviously woke him from his nap. He looked at Candice in disbelief. He'd pushed her buttons plenty of times in the past, but she's never screamed at him before.

"Lil' Man, go get your bag and let's go," Taleed said to his son and then turned to Candice. "See, I thought we was cool. I guess not." Then he walked out with his son following.

Taleed knew Candice was hiding her knowledge of Nicolas being in town, but he didn't press her any further. He didn't much care about what had happened to Nicolas. He wasn't hired to investigate Nicolas' demise, and as far as Taleed was concerned, Nicolas got just what he needed, a single shot in the chest.

Chapter 31

That next day, Taleed went to his parent's home to pick up his son. He and Kendra were going to spend the day with him.

"Go and get your bag," Taleed said to his son when he walked inside of his parents home. The young lad was pushing a red fire engine toy truck around the family room. Mrs. Mitchell, Taleed's mom, was busy cooking dinner and his father was in the rec room puffing on a cigar. *I'll check on pops before I leave.* Taleed made a mental note to himself. Mrs. Mitchell turned from the stove and smiled at her only son.

"Did he give you any trouble?" Taleed asked her because he knew that at times his son could be a handful, especially for someone as old as his parents. But as grandparents, they insisted on having their grandchild stay with them at least one weekend a month. Taleed made every attempt to make that happen.

"He's no trouble at all."

"Cool. Let me check in on pops before I head out." He walked down to the rec room where his father was puffing on a cigar and watching the evening news.

After making small talk, Taleed went to his old room where his son was sitting on the floor still playing with that same red fire engine toy truck.

"Hey Daddy, Mommy was screamin'." He pushed the toy truck back and forth on the hardwood floor. It made a loud siren sound.

Taleed ignored his rambling. "Boy, didn't I tell you to get your bag?" He was becoming irritated, and the noise from the toy fire engine added to his annoyance.

"She was screamin' real loud. Yellin'."

"What are talking about? Look Li'l Man, take this and this and put it in your bag," he said while handing his son some pajamas and his slippers. The young lad ignored him and continued his rant.

"Daddy, I was sleep but all the screamin' woke me up. Never heard Mommy scream like that."

"What? What are you talking about?" Taleed knelt down.

"Mommy was screamin' at that man."

"Oh." Taleed was finally able to decipher and listen to what his son had been saying. "Your mommy was yelling at somebody?" His son was trying to tell him about something he witnessed between his mother and someone else.

"No, screamin'. She was screamin' at that man."

"Oh. At who?"

"That man."

"Mr. Woody? Was your mommy screaming at Mr. Woody?" Taleed thought it was a bit odd because Candice and Woody had become fairly close after he moved in the multi-family unit. She wouldn't be screaming, but he could see how their conversation could be elevated and misinterpreted by his young son.

"Un-Un. Nic. Mommy was screamin' at Nic, real loud. She don't like that man."

"What about?" This time he had Taleed's full attention. If Nicolas was in town, then Candice lied to him.

"Un. I dunno."

Oh so now you got amnesia. Taleed thought to himself. "Get your hat, boy. Time to go."

Instead of going straight to confront Candice, Taleed dropped his son at DaRon's home. He wanted to talk to Candice.

When she opened the door, Candice was wearing shorts and a pink tank top. Her hair was pulled back in a ponytail. "Where's little Taleed?" she asked.

"He's with a friend." He closed the door after walking in and said, "We gotta talk. Me and you."

"What is it now?" Clearly she was frustrated, and it showed.

"Why you lie to me, young?"

"What are you talking about now, Taleed?"

"Last night?" He shrugged his shoulders and waited for an answer. She turned away. "When I asked you if you knew your boyfriend was in town. That's what I'm talk'n bout."

"That wasn't a lie. I didn't know Nic was here."

"Your son knew he was here because apparently the two of you had words. You want to change your story?"

"He came up Friday." Nicolas' unclaimed lifeless body is now resting in the city morgue.

Taleed rubbed his head thinking she might have some knowledge of his demise. He said, "And?"

"I really didn't know he was coming up. We got into it over something silly, and I guess we got kind of loud."

"Like what? Candice tell me what's going on? You can trust me. I mean after that shit dat went down in North Carolina, we was cool then."

She looked down, lowered her voice and said, "I know. But I don't want to say."

Without saying anything, Taleed stared at her making her a bit uncomfortable. "I guess I finally realized that Nic has a hot temper. He was still upset about my last visit."

"He ain't got no fucking hot temper. He just like to beat up on women. Why didn't you call me Candice?"

"For what, Taleed? Every time you do something to him he takes it out on me. So-so-so he was like, 'I'm here, where's your baby daddy.' I just wanted him to leave me alone. But he kept picking with me and picking with me." Tears flowed down her cheek.

"Naw, I think you leaving something out." Taleed doubted her story.

Candice finally gave in and told him what she should have told him when he and DaRon had to drive to North Carolina to find her beaten up by Nicolas. "The last time I went home, I told him I was pregnant, alright? I told him what I did and he wasn't happy. That's why he beat me up that night then, and I guess he wanted to finish me off. He was so-so mad. And I was scared of him."

"Hell, I don't know what happened next. I mean it happened. It just happened." She walked toward Taleed and placed her head in the middle of his chest. And just as she expected, he caressed her back trying to ease her pain, but it seemed like her shaking got even worse.

"He wasn't happy about becoming a father, huh?"

She pulled away from him, "He was not going to be a father! No, I wasn't about to have another child by another man who I wasn't in love with. That's not why he was angry. He didn't like it because I chose to do away with his unborn child. The nerve of him to accuse me of choosing what was right for me and not him. I decided what was right for me. For me, Taleed, not him but me!" Then she said, "I'm so scared, Taleed." Holding both her arms, Taleed looked down at her and stared into her eyes. She was still shaking as she looked away but he forced her to look at him.

"You scared?" So many thoughts ran through his mind. *Why was she scared? What did she have to fear? What had she done to be afraid of?* "What the fuck you gotta be scared about?"

"I-I don't want to go to jail. I can't be away from my son. He needs me. I need him, Taleed. You don't know what it's like to have your child control your life. Everything I do is because of little Taleed. I can't lose him. I would die. Please help me."

"Ah shit!" Taleed's eyes rolled upward and his head begin to spin thinking back to the time when his best friend Quintin was caught in the alley with a rival drug runner. The guy didn't have a weapon but Quintin did, and Quintin knew that if the other guy got out of the alley alive, he wouldn't have lasted another day. When Quintin came to Taleed's house he was sweating and shaking profusely. That was his first murder, and he was barely seventeen years old.

"Damn! Nicolas' body was found Saturday morning." Candice fell to her knees and cried like a baby. In shock, Taleed placed both hands on the top of his head. *Did she shoot that fool?* He reached for her and attempted to help her to her feet. When she stood, Candice wrapped her arms tightly around his waist.

"Don't leave me. Please don't leave me, Taleed." Taleed walked to the couch with her hanging on to him where the two sat. He tried to console her for what seemed like hours.

After she gathered some composure she slowly pulled away and looked at him with tear-filled eyes. Somewhere deep down, Taleed had a soft heart for her. He actually felt sorry for what she must have gone through that night. She stared at him waiting for him to scold her, but he didn't. Taleed instead sat upright and pushed her back against the couch.

"You can trust me, Candice I swear to you, you can trust me."

Candice then said, "Woody said we'll keep what happened between the two of us."

During the background check that DaRon had Taleed perform on Woody before he moved into the multi-family unit, there was nothing in his past that suggested his character was suspect. His record was clean, so Taleed knew that if he had anything to do with some kind of cover-up, his intentions were sincere. He felt that if she had something to do with his death, she had to have help with it in some manner. Woody had always treated Candice as if she were a daughter, and the good thing is Taleed's son liked him as well.

"Wait a minute. Wait a minute. Who heard this argument between you and Nicolas? Where was that chick from the university?" Taleed asked, referring to the University of Maryland grad student who resided in the apartment on the top floor.

"She wasn't here. She don't usually come in till after midnight." There were no other tenants in the unit.

He spoke slowly. "Candice, if you want me to help you, you have to tell me everything that happened that night." In between tears she told Taleed how Nicolas drove up from North Carolina and got to her apartment at 7 p.m. that night. He barged in, threatening to beat her up again because she stopped taking his calls. After about a few minutes of him pushing and shoving her around, Woody came up, but since she wouldn't let him inside, he convinced her to step out into the common area. Candice said that Woody had already given her a small weapon, so he told her to get it and stick it inside the pocket of her sweatshirt. He had also been taking her to the gun range regularly so that she could learn how to properly use it. She paused to say, "That's were we go every other Saturday."

That explains why Taleed kept seeing the two together. Candice continued to say that Woody's final

266

instructions to her were to use it if Nicolas hit her. Fifteen minutes later, she used it and ran to Woody's apartment where he told her to stay.

"You left my son alone?"

"He was asleep, Taleed."

"No he wasn't. He heard you yelling with that bitch."

Candice placed her head in her hand and sobbed. That night she and Taleed shared a secret that would be carried to their grave; a secret that Taleed would not share even with his best friends. He owed her that much. There was no way he would report what happened to the police and have his son's mother taken away from him, eventually ruining her life. Nicolas had already caused Candice enough pain in their relationship and no amount of ass whooping from Taleed was going to make the physical abuse she endured and her internal scars vanish. That night she had reached her limit. The cover-up was a crime, but what she did to protect herself was self-defense. Women around the world are battered every day by the hands of husbands and boyfriends. Unfortunately, Candice thought this behavior was acceptable and suffered through the pain until it finally got the best of her. In the end, Nicolas paid the ultimate price for his rage against this helpless woman.

Chapter 32

Chaz was reclining in the winged armchair as he stared out of the elongated window of the satellite office at the many lights and landmarks that lined the city.

L'Enfant was one of the greatest engineers to design and layout a city. He was a brilliant man in his time, stubborn but brilliant. It is truly amazing how one man could design a city as beautiful as the Nation's Capital and at the same time fight with and cause so much controversy between city officials and government administrators over the smallest detail. That fight was never resolved, and L'Enfant went to his grave not only a lonely man but also a broke one.

It had been a long day and now his brother's company was officially being traded on the New York Stock Exchange, and the first day's stock was a huge success.

Champagne was flowing, and everyone was going to walk away with a great return on his or her investments. During the celebration, the team was genuinely happy because of the long grueling process the staff from Keon-Chance Technology and their attorneys had gone through; everyone but his brother Chance. Chaz was well aware of why Chance was aloof during the entire time. KC was noticeably missing from the festivities. *My next mission is to get those two fools back on track.* Chaz thought, referring to Chance and KC's alienated friendship.

"There was no one at the front entrance." He wasn't expecting anyone at this time of the night.

"I sent everyone home," Chaz said in a solemn voice. It was not easy dealing with loneliness during a time when he should be the happiest man alive. He had just earned billions of dollars for his investors, his brother's company was now publically trading and his own company was doing well. But during this time of bliss, he had no one to share this moment with.

"And you, when are you going home?"

"Is there something I can do for you, Jaxsen?" Rarely did he call her by her full name.

"I want to talk to you."

"If you don't mind, we just ended this day on a wonderful note with this public offering and I'm really not in the mood for the conversation you seem to be used to having these days."

"I made one of the biggest if not *the* biggest mistake of my life."

"Sometimes we have to deal with the mistakes we make. Life sometimes is just one big mistake after the next." Chaz had heard that so many times and many times had given the same response.

"It was poor judgment on my part letting you go Chaz."

"You made your choice."

"Chaz, I came to explain why I did what I did. Please listen to me."

"Nah, I think you said enough already—"

"I need you."

"No you don't, and you made it clear to me that we were not in a relationship and never will be. That you made perfectly clear to me and everyone within ear shot. Perfectly clear how you didn't want to be with me like I wasn't good enough. If you wanted to embarrass me, you did that in front of my employees, in front of Rocky." He stood and walked around his desk. "But it's funny how you had no complaints when your legs were wrapped around my neck. I tried so hard to spend time with you, and when I had to leave, I left you with a satisfying smile on your face, even when we weren't fucking like two bunny rabbits!"

"Chaz, would you please listen—

"No! You listen to me. I travelled miles to be with you, rearranged business plans to spend time with you. I even had Gennie change my schedule on multiple occasions just to be with you and even had flowers delivered to you that you returned. I get it!"

"No you don't. I was wrong. I thought you were in love with your ex-wife and didn't want to be subjected to the hurt your love for her would eventually cause me. I was wrong for thinking you still cared for her. I knew then that I loved you, but Chaz, I didn't want to mislead you or cause you to lose out on the opportunity to bring your family

272

together. I didn't want to interfere, to-to come between your family. I'm in love with you Chaz and I'm sorry for everything I did when I was last here." He watched her as tears began to build in her eyes.

"Chaz, I was afraid of being hurt, but most of all, afraid for you. I was afraid of hurting you." The tears commenced to fall steadily onto her cheeks. "I guess I was afraid of loving you the way you should be loved. Afraid of giving myself to you. I'm not afraid anymore, Chaz. I know I'm in love with you. I know I'll always be in love with you. I need you. You were that friend, that lover I always dreamed of having and I want that friendship back. I want you back in my life." He listened and let his heart soften to the exact spot where she left it, whole, wanting her unlike never before. Using his thumb, Chaz gently wiped the tears from her cheek. "I didn't mean any of those nasty words I said to you when I was last here. I was so emotional. Things have changed. I realized how much I was in love with you and for so many weeks, I ached for you. My heart hurt every night for you, Chaz. I could never stop thinking about you. Every morning I wake up with images of you in my head. I wake up to your smell on me. I love you and I know you love me."

He stared at her. There was something different about her now than when he last saw her. She marched in his office furious with him over a simple business transaction, and now she's in tears pleading for him to take her back. *What is wrong with this woman?* He asked himself while continuing his stare. The steady flow of tears kept falling. There was very little she could do to stop them. Jaxsen only wished she had brought some tissues to wipe the tears away or the snot that was running out of her nose. So she used the palms of her hand. Chaz must have read her mind because he reached behind him and retrieved the box of tissues from his desk.

I have never seen one person so emotional like this woman. Chaz thought. He extended his hand and helped to wipe the tears from her face, "You've gained some weight." She sniffed but then looked downward. Jaxsen was embarrassed and now at a lost for words. "Hey, hey. Not in a bad way." He lifted her head and stared in her bloodshot eyes. The more she wiped her eyes, the more the tears ran down her cheek. He couldn't quite figure out what changed about her. But as quickly as he was confused, he suddenly knew what it could be. "You're pregnant?" He knew the answer to that question. She had that glow that pregnant women have when they're carrying. *I remember my ex-wife being so emotional in her early months of pregnancy. What else would cause Jax to be on this emotional roller coaster? Why would she be gaining weight? What else would cause only her face to swell so quickly?*

"Yes." She blinked away the tears.

Chaz leaned on his desk and said, "I thought we were…I dunno…safe." He lowered his head trying to think back to when he didn't use protection. Suddenly his memory jarred. It was nine weeks ago. Jaxsen looked so sexy wearing nothing but one of his pullover shirts. He snuck behind her and gave her a hug before leaving for the gym. That one innocent hug turned into kissing and then fondling. Chaz remembered how he made love to her while she stood at the kitchen sink. She had to hold on to it for leverage. Smiling, he thought to himself, *one morning while in the kitchen before leaving for the gym, we had a little quickie. Unlike previous times, I wasn't thinking with the right brain, I made love to her without using protection.* "About nine weeks." He remembered the day it happened just as she had remembered.

"Un-huh." She smiled for the first time in a while. Happy that he remembered the private moment they shared, but she still couldn't stop the steady flow of tears. "I'm so sorry you have to find out about my situation this way. I've just never been -- I mean I just want you to be there, that's all. I think it's only right that you know about this and, and, it's not like I'm trying to hide it from you. Chaz, I'm not saying we have to get married I-I-"

"This is not *your* situation, it's ours. Jax, don't you know me by now? I will drop everything going on in my life to be with you. I told you this before, and I meant every word."

Jaxsen remembered when he proposed the option. Chaz had invited her out on his boat one evening. She recalled saying something about the view and how peaceful it was being on the Bay.

Then she remembered his words verbatim: *"The only reason I don't spend all my time on the Bay is because I never had anyone to spend my life with who wanted this, too. I make millions in the investments, and could easily hire an analyst to do the legwork and only sit in on the board meetings so I can spend as much time as I want enjoying this view. Say the word and I can make it happen."*

She wondered how she could be so stupid ending their relationship and now she was fighting a losing battle with her tears. After hearing how he felt about her, she decided to let them fall along with the heavy heaving, she stood there shaking, unable to move.

"C'mere." He spoke softly and waited. But her legs betrayed her, they wouldn't allow her to move one inch, that is, until he reached out to her. When she walked into his arms, Chaz used his fingers to stroke her hair before asking, "Do you mean to tell me, I'm going to be a father, again?"

"Un-huh." She nodded.

"Wow. Do you know how long I've been waiting for this?" Jaxsen shook her head. "I know you won't believe this but ever since I laid eyes on you at the

Hard Rock Café—you know where we first met. Yeah, ever since that time."

"Oh my goodness and I thought you were just another womanizer like your brother. I so, so misjudged you. Can you ever forgive me?"

"I already have. Baby I forgave you a long time ago."

She mouthed, "*I love you.*"

"You know what?" Chaz asked, "I hope it's a girl."

He was genuinely thrilled about her having his child and even more so that she had come back to him. Jaxsen didn't come back because she was pregnant, she wanted his forgiveness and only hoped that he didn't hold any of the words she hurled at him against her, and he didn't. He truly loved her at first sight.

Epilogue

Two months later ...

Jaxsen submitted her resignation to THG in New York after deciding to move in with Chaz so that they could together raise their unborn child. She was happy that she had made the right decision to let Chaz know about her pregnancy, instead of having a child without him on her own. It wouldn't be fair to either him or his child. Jaxsen is now enjoying her role as his fiancé and stepmom to Trinidad who was thrilled after hearing he was going to be a big brother.

"Any regrets?" Chaz stood behind her holding onto her waist as Jaxsen prepared herbal tea to calm the morning sickness. The couple had retuned from her monthly visit to the obstetrician. The ultrasound determined that mom and daughter are on the right track, and in less than twenty-one weeks they will be welcoming a new baby girl into the family.

"None." She smiled.

"Me either sweetheart."

"Yeah, you don't have to deal with morning sickness though. I just wish my stomach would calm down some."

"Only a few more weeks sweetheart. You can do it." Hearing the baby's heartbeat made his day, but that jubilation was short lived when Chaz saw his brother walk in from the door leading to the garage. He had summoned him to discuss his pending role on the seat of his company.

Usually these visits with his brother were happy visits, however; lately the two of them had been at odds over his business stance in his company and his troubled relationship with KC, his former friend and estranged CEO.

After exchanging greetings with Chance, she watched her fiancé walk into his home office with his brother following close behind. The slamming of the interior door caused her to jump from where she stood.

Chaz started, "You two need to sit your asses down and hash this mess out before shit hit the fan."

"KC is a stubborn man. You know how he can be."

"What are you, ten? This is your fucking business, man! The one thing I said to you many years ago when you started this business is don't let the friendship get in the way of business. You took that advice and it did well for your company. When we talked about you removing KC from his duties, I said to not let the business relationship end your friendship. Now look at you. Look at you."

"I don't even wanna deal with that bullshit right now."

"You goin hafta deal with it! He's about to get hit with a big-ass lawsuit if he don't get his act together, and I'm not talking nickels and dimes either. By the time they get done with him, KC won't have a fucking pot to piss in. And you wanna know somethin', I'll be leading the troops cause I put my reputation on the line."

"Then talk to him."

"No! You talk to him. You know damn well how bad this could get for him and it could bring you and Tech down, too. I know one damn thing for sure, he ain't fucking over me." After dialing his number, Chaz spoke without waiting for a greeting. "Yo, dude. Your vacation is over. I expect you to be at my house in 15 minutes."

Chaz reclined in his huge office chair, crossed his legs on top of the desk and stared at his brother. Chance was slouched in the chair staring up at the ceiling. Without having to say a word, Chaz knew his brother was regretting this moment. He said, "What you whining about? Look, I spent nearly two hours at the gynie with my fiancé and you don't hear me whining. Both y'all acting like little hormonal bitches."

KC had been expecting the call he'd received from Chaz. He was also hoping to put off the meeting for at least another week or two. He glanced at Shaeterra who he had been spending a great deal of time with. Things had calmed down significantly in his life in the past three months, by intent. KC was working on fixing the wrongs in his life and Shaeterra was the perfect girlfriend standing by his side. *Almost perfect*, KC thought and then added, *I still ain't getting no ass. But that's aiight. I gotta respect her wishes. Things are different for me now, and I'm really feeling my Shae-Shae.*

"Hey, babe. I gotta go," he told her.

"Why? What's up, KC? Thought we were hanging out?" After hearing this, Shaeterra was slightly disappointed. She always looked forward to their time together.

"I know, I know." He walked to where she stood and cupped both cheeks in his hands. He knew Shaeterra was disappointed. "Time to get back to work." He kissed her lips and walked out.

When KC walked inside of his home office, Chaz was sitting behind his desk bouncing a ball of multi-color rubber bands against it. He looked up and said, "First thing Monday morning your ass will be walking through the doors of KC Tech and resuming your duties as CEO. There'll be some investors and board members hanging around for another three to six months. But you need to become familiar with all of them. Now sit yo ass down." Chaz stood. "Talk." He turned to Chance and pointed. KC had not noticed his friend's presence before. "Just because your company is public doesn't mean your role has diminished. You guys still play a pivotal role there at the office. That's your company. Now get it back. You figure out your role as controlling member and you," he pointed to KC, "figure out your new role as CEO. That has to be presented to the new team before midday. By that time, Rocky will be there to provide any legal advice," he said while walking towards the door. Then stopped and added, "And while you're at it, kiss and make up."

Both Chance and KC stared at each other without speaking. Chance knew his friend wasn't going to open his mouth so he stood and walked towards the oversized desk. He sat on the edge of it and asked, "Were you really going to start your own company?"

KC smacked his lips and said, "Man, I was blowing off a little steam, that's all." They both chuckled and once again it was silent for a moment.

"I hear you gotcha self a little sweetheart who's keeping you tame."

"Something like that." He smiled thinking of his relationship with Shaeterra and how it was so different from his other relationships.

"You get your problem fixed? With that girl?"

"Ya know, shit has a way of working itself out and in this case it was for the best. But hey, I'm working on a better me right now." He didn't know exactly what Taleed had done, he only knew Alex would no longer be a thorn in his side. KC stood and walked closer to Chance. He said, "Man, that was a misunderstanding that went way too far. I should have just listened in the beginning and we wouldn't be here."

Chance stood and held out his hand. "It's all good." The two friends shook hands and embraced. "Let's get outta here and get a drink."

Taleed was on another stakeout, but this time it was a matter of watch and wait when his cell phone vibrated. His first thought was to send the call to voice mail but he decided not to. He was dealing with a delicate situation with Candice and didn't want the slightest transgressions to set her off. Candice was an emotional wreck after what happened between her and Nicolas; she needed him to be there to help her cope with the situation. Taleed especially didn't want her to lose her mind and start running her mouth to the wrong people. Not only her but him and Woody could end up in a lot of trouble and Taleed was not about to let that happen. So to keep her in line he had been splitting his time between her home and spending time with Kendra. Needless to say, after finding out about it, Kendra didn't like that idea. Especially after hearing that he was spending two and sometimes three nights a week with Candice. Even though he camped out on her sofa, Kendra wasn't buying it and he understood. In fact, his dilemma was causing all sorts of jealousy from her, but he was dealing with it in his own way. He had to; Taleed was in too deep in his feelings for Kendra.

"Wassup?" he answered not taking his eyes off the entrance of the building.

"When are you coming back?" he held the phone away and stared in disbelief at the display. It was Kendra.

Taleed thought about their conversation earlier that morning when she accused him of being with Candice. He had stayed with Candice as long as he could before leaving at two in the morning to be with Kendra. Instead of her usual greeting she was seething when he walked inside. *"I smell her all over you!"* That was first time she had yelled at him. But if Kendra was going to be with him, she'd have to accept his arrangements, at least for a while. He wasn't about to let her dictate how he chose to deal with his son's mother. This morning, he'd left the warmth of her bed only hours ago telling her that he would return in less than an hour. The release was taking longer than expected.

"I got busy."

"Are you with her, Taleed?" Kendra whined almost in tears.

"Yo, stop it! When I ain't wit you, I'm working! I ain't hearin' this shit eve'r time you call, aiight? I'll call you when I'm on my way," he told her and then ended the call.

After tossing his cell phone on the dash, Taleed exited the vehicle and stretched out, reclining under the gazebo located in the center lot at Doctors Hospital. He was watching a nurse wheel the female's frail body through the sliding doors towards an awaiting cab. Bandages covered her head and one arm was in a cast. Gingerly, she stood and leaned forward, positioning herself to sit in the back seat. Alex didn't look like the same woman who befriended KC that night at the club where she was a waitress. Her face was swollen, eyes blackened and she'd lost some weight. *You sho can pick 'em.* He thought. Taleed knew one sure thing about his friend, KC was weak when it came to women, but he was no fool. KC was smart enough to know how psychotic Alex was and after only one date, he dumped her. But unfortunately for her, she refused to go away.

When I need some'n done right, I know who da call on, Gavin, Quintin's half brother. He flew just barely under the radar. That dude did enough damage in the eyes of the law but not considered illegal. And even if it was illegal, Gavin was too slick to get caught. He was there the night I did a personal favor for Victor. One evening I had spotted Victor's girl with her ex goin' inside a crack house. But it wasn't her being unfaithful, the ex was using their daughter as a pawn. I got my girl K to put on this hot-ass outfit and with Gavin they went in there spraying bullets. That's what I heard. I couldn't think of a better person to do what I needed done that night.

A slight smile formed across his lips as he thought to himself, *Good job, Gavin.*

Alex had lost her apartment because she had been laid up in the hospital for three months and being out of work, she had no money to pay her rent. The hospital paid for the cab ride but she had nowhere to go but to a battered women's shelter. Alex hadn't been battered. She was intentionally run over by an unknown motorists who she couldn't identify nor could she tell law enforcement what had happened to her that night when she was found near death on the side of Powder Mill Road. She had no recollection of the events that transpired that night. And even if she did remember, Alex had a strange feeling that what happened to her was not an accident. There were things that didn't make sense. That her car was vandalized in an affluent neighborhood was suspicious enough. The driver in the SUV that showed up at a moment when she most needed was no coincidence. She was probably targeted because of her inability to accept rejection from men. She had a jealous streak when it came to many, and any man who paid attention to her, she wanted all to herself. In her mind, she thought what happened to her must have had something to do with KC, her latest love interest. She had seen him plenty of times in the club with multiple women. But at the time, that didn't matter to her, she was out to have him all to herself. Out of all the men she met at the club, he was the most attentive and when after one night together, he rejected her, she couldn't let him go. Alex was in love, so she thought. Nevertheless, in a cruel way this accident was a reminder of how city life was a far cry from the way life was back home in that small town of Pleasant Hill, Louisiana. Maybe it's time to go back there because ending up alone on the side of a dark street isn't the reason she left her home, but it's a strong enough deterrent to make her want to return.